Bidding on a Second Chance

A SMALL TOWN CHRISTIAN ROMANCE

CHRISTMAS IN REDEMPTION RIDGE

EMILY CONRAD

Copyright © 2023 by Emily Conrad

Published by Hope Anchor, LLC

PO Box 3091, Oshkosh, WI 54903

Library of Congress Control Number: 2023917724

This is a work of fiction. Names, characters, places, and incidents are either the products of the series authors' imaginations or are used fictitiously. Any resemblance to actual persons, living or dead, businesses, or actual events is purely coincidental. Any real locations named are used fictitiously.

ISBN 9781957455136 (Paperback Edition)

ISBN 9781957455136 (Ebook Edition)

Edited by Brandi Aquino, Editing Done Write

Proofread by Judy DeVries, Judicious Revisions

Cover designed by Amanda Walker, PA & Design Services

Author photograph by Kim Hoffman

Visit the author's website at EmilyConradAuthor.com.

To anyone whose Christmas would be a little brighter with a puppy and a second chance.

Emily Conrad

Chapter One

The moment Graham Lockhart glanced at his phone, all his experience navigating crises failed him. The bustling grocery store checkouts disappeared from around him, and his vision tunneled down to one name: Piper Wells.

Other than Sunday mornings, when they both attended Redemption Bible Church, Piper hadn't tolerated being in the same room with him since she'd refused his marriage proposal two years ago. Even at church, she never so much as looked at him.

Now she had texted?

A troubling blend of skepticism and hope—hope for what, he couldn't even say—tightened his mouth and jammed up his breath. He tapped the notification.

I promise this is not as big of a deal as it sounds, but I can't come to dinner. I'm at the walk-in clinic because I was hit by a pickup.

A grunt escaped his throat.

Another message appeared below the first. *But seriously, no alarm. Nothing vital was broken.*

He prided himself on being able to see through the half-truths and outright lies he encountered as a police officer. In emergencies, he knew what to do, when, and how. But Piper's messages left him as confused as a university-level logic puzzle. Should he worry? Brush it off? Skimming the words a second time, he checked off facts.

He hadn't had dinner plans with her since the fateful night at Ridgeline Grill when she'd severed their relationship for reasons he still didn't believe. Therefore, the message wasn't intended for him.

If she'd checked in at a walk-in clinic, rather than the emergency room, she hadn't been transported by ambulance. Yet his muscles tensed at the phrase *I was hit*. Did she mean her vehicle or her body had taken the blow?

Based on her specification that *nothing vital was broken*, he guessed something she deemed not vital *had* been. Though any car accident could cause injuries, the likelihood skyrocketed in a pedestrian-versus-vehicle impact. His stomach churned at the idea of Piper—petite, beautiful Piper—in such danger.

A cart bumped his groceries, and the noodles he'd purchased for tonight's lasagna rattled. A girl of eight or nine peered over the handlebar and shouted an apology. The mom added a regretful smile as the pair left with a swish of the doors.

"My own fault." But they were already gone. Graham moved out of the center of the walkway but, in the process, stepped on someone's foot.

"Easy there, Graham." A hand landed on his shoulder. He turned to find retiree Chaz Buchanan's silver eyebrows tented with concern. The man had moved to Redemption Ridge to help on his brother's ranch a few years ago and had quickly become a part of the community. "Everything okay?"

Graham's focus dropped back to Piper's message. Her fine features and small build had inspired protectiveness in him from the first time he'd met her, when she'd caught her foot on the corner of a display in this very store. She'd always been accident-prone, but this incident, whatever the details were, took it to a whole new level. His body stood on edge at the idea of a truck even getting close to her. The driver had better hope Graham never learned his identity, or he'd be in for a lifetime of speeding tickets and whatever else Graham could catch him at. No leniency.

"Graham?"

He blew out a breath and surveyed the store to bring himself back from the brink of a vendetta. He probably shouldn't look up the incident report.

But what to say to Chaz? The man had recently found love and might have sound advice to offer, but Graham's breakup with Piper was the stuff of Redemption Ridge legend. It wasn't every day people witnessed a proposal—let alone a refusal. He never should've chosen to pop the question in a popular restaurant, but he'd learned his lesson. He refused to reignite the rumors by mentioning her now.

Not that Chaz would spread it around, but Agnes Hawthorn, a waitress who served up at least as much gossip as food, would. She finished paying for her basket of groceries and headed their way.

"Sorry, Chaz. I just got a notification about an accident that requires my attention." He offered a polite smile and made a quick exit.

The text did require attention. The question was, what kind? He could call the station and ask about the accident. Or he could check on Piper himself.

She may have done the equivalent of running over his heart with a pickup, but he didn't wish her harm.

He was a public servant, under oath to protect and serve. He ought to make sure she had handled the incident correctly. See to it that she, a citizen of Redemption Ridge, Colorado, made it home safely.

He sent a reply. *Which clinic?*

Chapter Two

Crutches. Again.

Piper had been forced to rely on the contraptions twice before—no, wait, make that three times. Pastor spoke sometimes about God's protection and loving care, but she always struggled to understand how that fit with days like today.

"Got it?" The nurse opened the exam room door.

She nodded, adjusting her balance. What she didn't have was a ride home, and she needed to get there as soon as possible. Teddy was there alone, and her nephew, Bryce, was due in an hour. Unfortunately, Lucy, her best friend, hadn't answered her request for a lift.

Despite her desperation, she wouldn't let Grandma and Grandpa rescue her, if such a thing could be helped. After Mom and Dad died in an accident when she was nine, her grandparents had raised her and her older brother, but the elderly couple didn't get around well anymore. She shouldn't have answered their query about which clinic she'd come to. She hobbled out to the waiting room, the crutch rubbing her sore arm and side with every step. What a wreck. At least no white-haired retirees awaited her.

Who could she call on for a ride? Piper eased into a seat and sent a prayer heavenward. The incident in the parking lot of Charlie's Hardware had fractured her phone screen into an intricate spiderweb of glass. She scrolled through her contacts, straining to read names through the broken display.

Someone approached, so Piper shifted her crutches to clear the walkway. The person stopped and cleared a masculine-sounding throat. Worn brown work boots stood, one visible on either side of her phone. Jeans. Canvas jacket open over a thermal shirt. Square jaw. Blue eyes the shade of distant mountains. Mop of curly brown hair, begging for her fingers.

Graham.

Attraction, no more welcome than the truck had been, slammed into her.

Lord, please, I need a break.

The pain in her foot chided her to make her prayers more specific.

Rest. I need rest. And protection from more pain.

How had her ex heard about the accident? Probably from Cody, his best friend, who'd been first on the scene. She clutched her phone tighter and shifted her injured foot back, partially under her chair. As if Graham, an expert at spotting details, wouldn't have noted the clunky black brace the moment he'd walked in.

"What are you doing here?" she asked.

Stubborn smugness replaced his concern. Though more irritating, the expression made him no less handsome. "You texted me."

"No, I didn't."

"Wanna bet?" His lips twitched with the smile that used to make it easy to forgive his teasing. Too easy.

Her fingers flew over her phone screen. Because of the

condition of the surface, navigating to her sent messages took three times longer than normal. "I only texted Lucy and Grand—"

Oh no. Not Grandma. *Graham*. Her face flamed. Distracted by pain and the broken screen, she'd selected the wrong name.

She blinked hard. She'd expected to see more of Graham soon because of her plan to get her nephew back on the straight and narrow, but *see* had been the operative word. She hadn't planned to interact with him, even on her best day— which was *not* today.

She reread the message to avoid looking up—the more she looked at him, the harder it would be to maintain emotional distance. "This obviously wasn't meant for you."

"And being hit by a truck isn't a 'no alarm' situation. You aren't driving yourself home." Calm, cool, and in control, this was the Graham she'd fallen in love with.

The Graham she would never allow back into her heart.

As if he wanted back in.

She peeked at him. The stubble covering his jaw—not to mention the casual clothes—meant he was off today. The narrowing of his smoky-blue eyes meant she was a problem to solve. One he might be willing to solve by sweeping her off her feet, but only literally and only if he saw it as the quickest means to getting on with his day.

"I'll figure it out."

Graham remained as unmoved as the mountains that formed a backdrop for the town. "You didn't drive yourself here."

"Jason Keen happened to be at the store. He drove me." The flashing lights of the ambulance and the police cruiser had drawn a lot of attention, probably resulting in the best day of sales Charlie had experienced in years. Maybe he'd give her a discount next time she went in for supplies. Except it'd be a while before she was in shape to refinish any more furniture to sell in her secondhand clothing and home goods store, Second Chances. The delay would put her weeks behind schedule.

Weeks she didn't have.

Graham shifted, and her gaze, like a persistent homing pigeon, flitted to his face again. "If Jason drove you here, you don't have your car. Even if you did, the good citizens of Redemption Ridge don't deserve to be subjected to you driving with your left foot on the pedals."

She shuddered at the idea, and her cheeks notched a few degrees hotter.

"Did you report this to the police?"

"Of course." She hadn't wanted to. In a town this size, with only a handful of officers, it'd been far too likely Graham would respond to the call. Then she'd gone and texted him herself.

"How did it happen?"

"I was blindsided." Usually people meant the word figuratively, so using it literally was funny, right?

Apparently not. Graham crossed his arms, a silent demand for a better answer. She'd never seen him question a suspect, but she had no doubt he excelled at getting the information he needed. He wouldn't leave before he got answers.

"The driver was turning. He said there was a little boy on the other side of the lane. He was so busy keeping an eye on him that he never even saw me. Which makes no sense to me, because I swear he looked right at me, but this is kind of how my life goes." Even shrugging helplessly—or was it hopelessly? —demanded an inordinate amount of energy.

"Were there witnesses?"

"One. Cody got his statement."

Graham flinched. Cody must not have mentioned the accident after all. "What's the diagnosis?" He lifted his chin to indicate her foot.

With sweater weather firmly upon them, she could keep him from glimpsing her skinned elbow and the deep purple blooming on her arm. If he witnessed her moving, he might guess the bruised rib, but she wouldn't be the one to tell him. Better for him to think her foot was the only injury. It hurt worse, anyway. "I can't walk on it. They say it isn't broken, but a specialist will take another look after the weekend. Tuesday or Wednesday."

"They couldn't get you in sooner?" He worked his jaw and glared toward the check-in desk like he might turn a bad cop routine on the unsuspecting receptionist.

"The specialist only comes to Redemption Ridge twice a week."

He frowned. "How long to heal?"

"They think it'll be a week or two, and I'm good with crutches. It's fine." A bluff. She wanted to collapse into her armchair, pull up a blanket, position a couple of ice packs, and not move for a month. Unfortunately, if she did that, her business would tank, and she'd let down a local family who was counting on her.

"It's not fine." Graham couldn't know everything she had on her plate, but the way he assessed her said he had a rough idea of how little time she had for injuries of this magnitude. If it weren't for their history, she would've sworn she saw kind concern swimming laps in those blue irises of his. "You were hit by a truck."

The seriousness of it crept up on her, pushing forward tears she hadn't realized were so near the surface. She willed them back, but her sniffle made Graham's mouth tighten again. If she wanted to pull something over on him, she'd have to try harder. She rallied a smile. "If it's not fine, it's at least par for the course. A day in the life of Piper Wells."

His frown deepened. "I'm giving you a ride home."

She was stranded, and he knew it. And the only reason he

knew it was because she'd been flustered enough to send him a message telling him so.

She squirmed under the intensity of his gaze. He'd always been good at making her feel like the only woman in the world, and his skill hadn't faded in the last two years. Perhaps he'd been practicing on someone else? Yes. That must be it. Someone not from Redemption Ridge, or she'd have heard about it.

"Let's go."

She was sore and tired, and Teddy needed her. The fastest way home was Graham. As a professional knight in shining armor, he was obligated to keep insisting until she allowed him to assist her. She'd never liked being a damsel in distress, but the Lord had once again assigned her the role, and she didn't have the energy to keep arguing. "Fine, but only because someone else is depending on me."

Graham helped her to her feet with a surprisingly gentle hand under her good arm. The impulse to lean against his chest and let those arms encircle her was so magnetic that resisting the compulsion tipped her dangerously in the opposite direction. He caught her waist and wrapped a protective arm around her shoulders, saving her from falling by pulling her into the exact embrace she'd been trying to avoid.

From their first date onward, his hugs had always felt more like home than she'd experienced anywhere else since she'd lost her parents. Somehow, that sense of safety and belonging hadn't shattered along with their relationship. Forget curling up in the armchair for a month. She could—

The softness of his thermal shirt against her cheek registered. Regardless of how right this felt, it *wasn't* right. She sucked in and held a breath, freezing until she could regain her bearings. And her self-control.

So the guy was attractive. And kind. And had amazing reflexes.

None of that negated the fact that they didn't want the same things out of life. A relationship would never work long-term. Since she forever struggled to keep that front and center in her heart, she inventoried other obstacles between them: he was bossy, Bryce hated him, he worked an undeniably dangerous job. Plus, she'd once ended up with stitches because he'd left a cabinet open.

That last one was petty, but if it kept her from throwing herself into his arms at every opportunity, so be it.

"You good?" Graham's chest shifted like he was peering down at her.

She straightened.

He moved back as one might step away from a tower of playing cards. An accurate metaphor for her physical state ... and the rest of her life too. Once she'd settled onto her crutches, he snagged her purse from the chair.

She extended a hand. "I'll carry that."

He motioned to the door without surrendering the accessory. Given his superior sense of balance and his workout regime, which had reduced her to a boneless puddle the time she'd tagged along, she was in no state to fight him on the courtesy. If the man wanted to carry a purse, he could carry a purse. And with the no-nonsense set of his jaw, no one was likely to raise any questions about it.

Outside, he escorted her to the passenger seat of his truck. Her crutches thumped into the bed of the vehicle, and he climbed behind the wheel. "You might want to text your grandparents about dinner."

"Oh!" She scrambled for the phone. "They probably have the food on the table and everything."

"I can take you there instead." Graham's low voice was as warm and toasty as a campfire.

This was dangerous ground. She would not fall for the man. She could not. For everyone's sake—especially his.

11

Chapter Three

How could Piper's nails remain perfect after a run-in with two and a half tons of steel? Graham locked his gaze on the road and didn't ask. She wouldn't have an answer, and she didn't need to know he paid her such close attention. She certainly didn't need to know he'd always considered her small hands and delicate fingernails, perpetually glossy with a clear coat, perfect. Any touch from her had always been far more jolting than it ought to be, and that spark wasn't her only superpower.

Her dark-brown irises and the slight downward curve of her lower lash line made her eyes look suited to a cartoon fawn. Combine those with her expressive eyebrows and her upturned nose and one glance from her could reach his heart faster than a bullet—and leave just as much carnage.

Her effect on him was empty chemistry. Superficial remnants of what had once been—or what he'd once thought they'd had, anyway.

Silence radiated toward him from the passenger seat. Why couldn't he move on like she had? He needed to forget about her, her hands, and the pesky instinct to offer help as she recovered.

He cleared the concern from his throat and replaced it with gruff detachment befitting their current relationship. "You can't do your job like that."

"I can do enough." Piper combed her fingers through her hair. The clip holding it back looked ... stressed. The thing had already let loose strands on either side of her face long enough to reach her collarbone. "I won't rearrange Second Chances' displays until after I'm back on my feet."

"That's a plan to fail if I've ever heard one." Sure, she'd always liked to keep the store fresh, but changing the look was optional.

Much of what she did wasn't.

Locals brought towers of clothing and accessories for her to evaluate. What she deemed stylish, she bought from them and resold. She also received deliveries of new home goods. While they'd dated, he'd regularly stacked the hefty boxes in the stockroom for storage until they were needed on the sales floor. She'd managed without him in the time since, but that was without an injured foot.

Piper exhaled an incredulous scoff. "I'm a competent business owner. I'll get by."

He may have taken the gruffness too far. Still. "You can't even drive. How will you get around?"

Piper's eyebrow rose, an indication that her temper was doing the same. "It's not like I did this on purpose."

"Right. I know. But what now?" He willed her to have a plan that would allow him to walk away.

Because he wanted to walk away.

Right?

Right. She'd dumped him heartlessly.

"I'll figure it out."

"Can Bryce help you?" She'd had custody of her nephew since shortly before breaking up with Graham.

"Bryce is ten."

"If he's old enough to skip school, he's old enough to help."

"You heard about that." Soft and filled with regret, her voice indicated she'd hoped he hadn't.

"Police give missing children top priority because sometimes, it's more serious than a boy walking away from recess to get a cupcake." Back in September, when the call came in, Graham spent an hour searching the streets of Redemption Ridge before word came over the radio that Bryce had turned up at The Cakery, asking what he could buy for the three dollars and six cents in his pocket. "Maybe extra responsibilities would be good for him."

"He's busy as it is. He has some homework and friends, of course, and he goes to church on Wednesday nights. Plus ..." She cleared her throat, but her next words came out mumbled. Something about basketball?

Graham's grip on the steering wheel tightened. When it came to basketball, he could imagine only one reason she'd try to slip something past him. "What was that?"

Her hand hovered by her mouth, but she enunciated this time. "Rec league basketball starts soon."

"He's enrolled?"

"Uh-huh."

"You haven't forgotten I'm one of the coaches."

"*Assistant* coach." The hand lowered, and her voice picked up speed and volume as she launched her defense. "But there are a few teams. Statistically, he had greater odds of *not* being on your team."

The roster had landed in Graham's inbox, but he hadn't bothered to read the names. He'd never considered Bryce might be among his players. One of the weak reasons Piper

14

had given him for their breakup was that Bryce resented him for arresting his father. Ryan had stolen a car and racked up a list of offenses to fuel a drug addiction—with his son in tow. His subsequent incarceration was the reason Bryce lived with Piper.

While the resentment was no doubt true, Graham believed they could've overcome it with enough time and patience. Piper hadn't given him the opportunity. "Was he assigned to me?"

"He was assigned to Kent Greely." The way she said the name indicated she already knew Graham was Kent's second-in-command. "I can't limit his options for activities just because I have an ex." Whether it was guilt or a plea for understanding that rounded her eyes, his defenses cracked.

This was his chance to disprove her assumption that he didn't have the insight to break through to her nephew. Besides, police work was rewarding, but volunteering with the youth basketball league allowed him to develop positive relationships with kids before they ever crossed paths with law enforcement. Bryce was exactly the kind of child Graham wanted to help.

He pulled into Piper's driveway and helped unload her crutches.

Hunched against them, she pushed back the wispy layers of light-brown hair that framed her face. The pink flush he'd noticed when she'd first spotted him in the waiting room returned. "I've got it from here. You've gone far enough out of your way."

He might agree, if only he hadn't seen the tremor in her fingers. "I'll see you up the stairs."

She frowned at the back of her house, where there were no stairs. The ones he meant were just inside the door.

Piper ascended the four steps into her kitchen with only one tenuous moment of wobbling. "Okay. I'm up the stairs."

She held out her hand for the purse again, and this time, he passed it to her. "I'm tired. I'm sore. I just want to—"

A yip sounded in the next room. A small yip. Followed by a little whimper.

"Since when do you have a dog?" The noises drew him into the kitchen. He knelt in front of the crate beside the cabinets. Two dark eyes peered out at him, and a tiny nose pushed against the metal grid that made the kennel's door. Graham opened it, and a fur ball tumbled into him. The puppy couldn't be more than two months old. "A labradoodle?"

Piper clipped a leash on the collar. "Come on, Teddy." She hobbled down the stairs at an impressive speed. Trying to prove something? Whatever the motivation, she'd risked her life, considering the boot and her track record.

Too bad for her the dog remained at the top, peering down as though she'd asked him to jump into a canyon teeming with coyotes.

"You can do it, buddy." She gave a gentle tug of encouragement.

Teddy's teeth clamped on the leash. He dedicated each of his fifteen-or-so pounds to yanking the opposite direction.

Piper exhaled her frustration, sending a lock of hair up in a puff. "

Graham scooped up the puppy and carried him outside, scrubbing his fingers through the wriggly dog's fur. "This is why you were concerned about getting home?"

Piper continued to hold the leash as Graham set the pup down. "He was in his kennel a lot longer than I meant him to be, and it's way past his dinnertime."

Teddy ambled around, sniffing, his light curls matching the driest blades of the November grass. "When did you get him?"

"Two days ago."

Graham eyed her brace. When he'd adopted Banjo, caring

for, training, and keeping the black lab out of trouble had taken every spare moment for months. "Puppies are a lot of work."

"I haven't had a good night's sleep since we brought him home."

If she'd been sleep deprived before she'd been hurt, she would have even more trouble now. Back inside, Piper scooped food into Teddy's bowl while the puppy sat, waiting.

"He looks like a stuffed animal. It's not right."

Piper smiled as she lowered the dish, and Teddy started chomping his kibble. "Too adorable for you? Afraid he'll blow your tough guy cover?"

Maybe. He *was* suppressing an urge to coo at the fluff ball. He fixed his line of sight on Piper but found himself slammed by yet another urge—to take care of her. He gulped. Hadn't he had enough abandonment to last a lifetime? He took a step toward the exit. Teddy romped in the opposite direction.

"Little stinker." Piper crutched after the puppy into the living room.

She did *not* have that under control.

When Graham reached the living room, the puppy was nowhere to be seen.

The soft scrape of fur against leather sounded to his right. He slid the couch from the wall and grabbed Teddy before the canine could sink his puppy teeth into a lamp cord. "Got any toys around here?"

Piper stepped toward the opposite end of the couch, where a wicker basket, already bearing telltale chew marks, held a collection of balls and stuffed toys. Graham motioned her to let him get it. He set the dog in front of a treat-stuffed ball, but even that wouldn't keep the gremlin busy long.

"I know what you're thinking," Piper said. "But I have friends. Lucy must've had something come up, but I'm sure she'll be free soon."

As a large animal vet, Lucy could be tied up with her duties on some remote ranch for hours. And even when she reached her own home on the outskirts of Redemption Ridge, she had her own animals to tend to.

Teddy lost interest in the toy and began chewing the coffee table. Graham redirected him. "When does Bryce come home?"

"Should be soon."

Then Graham wouldn't have to wait long for reinforcements. His stomach rumbled. If he'd gone home instead of to Piper's rescue, the lasagna he'd planned would be in the oven. He eyed his charge. "What's your plan for dinner?"

"I don't know. I'll think of something." She mumbled about a baked potato, but Graham was already in the kitchen.

If he was stuck on puppy duty until backup arrived, he'd cook while he waited. That would keep him away from Piper while allowing him to supervise the dog. He scanned the selection in the pantry and the refrigerator.

"Graham?" Piper's voice rose quick and worried.

When he stepped back into the living room, she pointed at Teddy, who'd returned to the leg of the coffee table. He scooped up the dog again. "Does this mean you're going to let me help?"

"You are an excellent cook."

He straightened, holding the wiggling dog by his side. "I didn't think you liked my cooking that much."

"Why not?"

"I could've been cooking for you for two years now." The remark was childish and immature. He heard it as soon as it was out.

Instead of rolling her eyes at him like he deserved, Piper leveled a glare. "When you weren't working."

"It wasn't the hours you had a problem with."

He could still play their breakup in his mind like a movie.

She'd followed him out of the restaurant after he'd tried to propose. When he'd suggested they could get past Bryce hating him, she'd started shaking her head like a leaf blowing in the wind. "Your job is dangerous, and I'm accident prone, and it's too much risk."

He'd been shocked, humiliated, and angry—too much to ask why his job, which he'd had for years before they'd started dating, was suddenly a problem. And why her being accident prone meant she thought they shouldn't be together. Why she didn't think she was safer with him than without.

No way he would've let her wander out in front of a pickup truck, that was for sure.

She shifted, jerked to a stop, and pressed a gentle hand to her side. Her movement must've aggravated some injury. "You're right. It wasn't your hours. But let the record show my concern also wasn't your cooking." She shook her head and looked away. "As if people get married for food."

"They get married because they love each other and want a family." What else could her excuses for the breakup amount to but a lack of love?

She flinched. "See if you can close the cabinets this time."

As if he hadn't apologized a million times for the mistake. He saw far worse than wounds that required three stitches on the job, but watching so much of Piper's blood stream from the gash on her forehead had left a permanent imprint. He'd taken great pains to never leave anything out of place as he cooked again. If he'd gotten any closer to wrapping her up in protective air bubbles, he would've suffocated her. "You know I feel terrible about that."

She frowned, the fight gone. "Right. Yes. I do. Sorry."

"Me too." He pushed his hand through his hair, trying to focus on the present. Rehashing the past would do nothing but stir up their worst. She didn't love him. He'd accept it and move on.

Maybe.

Someday.

"You've got the ingredients for risotto."

She gulped visibly and eyed him, as if to judge the sincerity of his apology. "I haven't had risotto since ..." She swallowed again. "In years."

She hadn't had it since he'd last made it for her, then.

Carrying the dog under his arm, he returned to the kitchen. He'd do Piper the favor of wearing out the dog while he worked. Hopefully, Bryce would wander in before the meal was finished. He'd have a quick talk with the boy about helping around the house, and then he'd be out of Piper's life again. For good this time.

Chapter Four

Hearing but not being able to see Graham in the kitchen made Piper's good leg bounce. Was there an inconspicuous way to move to the couch? He sure was telling the dog to sit a lot, but his voice was forever patient. Usually, after he said the command, he waited a moment, said, "Good dog," and then she'd hear a crunch or two.

Among the beats of their never-ending cycle, she heard cabinet doors, pans, the oven, and the microwave. He chopped something. When the sizzle and aroma of bacon rose, she couldn't resist any longer. She wrested her sore body from the armchair.

Graham appeared at the door, a glistening wooden spoon in hand. Teddy trotted at his heels, watching the spoon like it was a magic wand about to make all his dreams come true. "Did you need something?"

A better view. "An ice pack."

"I'll get it. Sit."

Teddy licked his chops and obeyed the command.

Choking on the cuteness, she motioned. Graham turned, and his burst of laughter brought the puppy to his feet. He took a piece of kibble from a small pile on the counter and passed it to the dog before retrieving the ice pack.

She settled on the couch, her bad foot on the cushions with the ice balanced on top.

Graham stood at the stove, the muscles of his shoulder blade shifting against his shirt as he stirred. Teddy stared up at him, looking every bit the stuffed animal Graham had said he appeared to be. The pair should not look that adorable or that well-suited to her kitchen.

This was not good.

She lowered her focus to her phone and texted Lucy.

Graham found out about the accident. He's insisting on taking care of me until someone else arrives. Tell me you're on your way!

Even as she sent it, she knew Lucy wasn't. If she'd gone this long without responding to any of Piper's messages, it meant some poor animal needed Lucy's help even more than Piper did. After all, Piper's biggest problem was the attractive —albeit frustrated—man in her kitchen, cooking for her and training her puppy.

The back door creaked. Piper checked the time. Of course her nephew had to be early tonight, of all nights. Plodding footsteps sounded on the stairs in the back hall. Bryce stepped into the kitchen, his look of confusion quickly transforming into betrayal when he recognized the man at the stove.

Graham, however, smiled. "Bryce, just the guy I wanted to see." At a pop, he turned his attention back to the risotto. He poured in a little more water and stirred. "Hungry?"

"No." But Bryce's eyes fixed on the pan. The aromas of bacon and onion could make a stick figure's mouth water. The plan had been for Bryce to come home for dinner. He wouldn't have eaten with the Snowdens, and the risotto had to tempt him.

She opened her mouth to intervene before something rude popped out of her nephew's mouth, but Graham stepped into Bryce's line of sight. "Your aunt was in an accident, and her foot was hurt. She's going to need a lot of help these next few weeks."

"Not from you."

"I guess that leaves you, then." Graham spoke with the same unflappable calm he'd used with Teddy. "This puppy needs someone to play with and take him outside and train him. Do you think you can handle that?"

Bryce eyed Teddy, who patrolled the edge of the stove for fallen bacon. More than half the reason they'd gotten the puppy had been Bryce's begging and his promises to help with everything Graham had listed. Her nephew's distaste lessened until he returned his focus to Graham. "You don't belong here."

Once again, Piper took a breath to tell Bryce to mind his manners, but then Graham spoke, voice still even and calm— but firm. "Piper loves you, and she does a lot for you. The least you could do—"

"If it weren't for you, no one would have to do anything for me." Bryce made a break for the stairs.

"Bryce." The ice pack tumbled to the ground as Piper rose, but the boy was already gone. To think she'd hoped interacting with Graham would smooth over some of Bryce's hard feelings about Ryan's incarceration.

His door slammed.

She put her bad foot down, but shooting pain made her lift it again. For balance, she leaned her knee on the couch. "I'm sorry, but you should go. I'll talk to him."

Graham let out a long, slow breath, peering after her

nephew. Finally, he angled the handle of the spoon toward her. "Add the water a little at a time. Stir constantly. When all the water is absorbed, this is done."

She stepped forward, and he showed himself out.

Chapter Five

At the mention of the Rasinskis, the four others in the office area of the station abruptly headed for the lobby. The phone tethered Graham to his desk, or he'd join them before they made quick work of whatever treats the owners of Donut Haven had brought by. He tried to signal Cody to set something aside, but his friend didn't spare him a glance.

Graham's stomach rumbled with impatience. "Yes, ma'am. I'll have a word with him about playing music at that volume, but—"

His elderly caller cut him off—awfully eager to speak for someone who wasn't reporting the noise complaint until hours after the neighbor had shut off his stereo. When he finally wrapped up the call, he headed after the others.

Cody, halfway through a vanilla donut caked in sprinkles, stood near Rebecca Rasinski.

Todd, her husband, lifted the one white paper bag the vultures hadn't taken off his hands. "It nearly cost me my life, but I saved your favorite. One glazed cinnamon twist."

"You are a true hero." Graham accepted the treasure with

both hands. Even without opening the crimped top, the scent of cinnamon set his mouth to watering. "If I fail my next fitness test, these are going to be to blame."

Laughing, Rebecca passed him napkins. "That'd be counterproductive, since this is a thank you. We've been dropping off deliveries around town, since we're just so grateful to everyone. Everywhere we turn, we see another flyer for the auction." She lifted her hand toward the community bulletin board in the station foyer.

A bright red-and-green poster extended a cheery invitation to the auction benefiting the Rasinski family on December twenty-third. Little Riley Rasinski had battled cancer, and all of Redemption Ridge had breathed a sigh of relief when she'd been declared cancer-free. Yet the disease had bottomed out the family's finances. If all went well, the donated items sold at the auction would put them back in the black. Then, they could officially close the painful chapter and move forward.

"We're all behind you. One hundred percent. In fact, what do we owe you for this delivery? It's worth at least thirty dollars."

"We should have you price everything for us." Todd laughed and waved him off. "Redemption Ridge has been good to us. More than we ever expected."

Graham unrolled the top of the bag, revealing the large, glazed cinnamon donut. The couple got pulled into conversation with other officers. Once they were gone, an elbow to his side interrupted before he got the donut from the bag.

Cody polished off the last of his treat, wiped a sprinkle from his lip, and tipped his head toward the flyer. "We have a problem."

When he didn't expand, Graham skimmed the poster. The date, time, and cover fee weren't the issue—he and Cody had bought tickets weeks ago. And then, he saw it. The advertisement promised *Second Chances signature refinished furniture, including a complete bedroom set.*

"Since when does Second Chances refinish furniture?" Back when he and Piper dated, he had sanded and repainted a china cabinet for her. She'd been amazed by the transformation, and they'd gone on to refinish a dresser together. Now she had incorporated the process he'd taught her into her business? He glanced at Cody. "Even without an injury, she's got a full plate raising her nephew, dealing with that puppy of hers, and running the store. When did she throw furniture into the mix?"

"A while ago." Cody turned.

Graham stepped into his friend's escape route. "How do you know that?"

The only way Cody's look of feigned innocence could become more conspicuous would be if he started whistling.

"You shop at her store?"

"My house was empty." Cody's shoulder lifted nearly to his ear with a helpless shrug. "I heard she'd started refinishing furniture and selling house stuff, so yeah, I went in."

About eight or ten months ago, Cody's living room furnishings had filled out with framed artwork, a storage chest, a couple of throw pillows, and a bookshelf with old military and aviation books. In comparison, Graham had begun to reconsider his own cheap, some-assembly-required furnishings.

"You ought to see the dressers and desks she does. She can't keep them in stock. I don't know how you didn't hear about it sooner."

"The whole town is on her side?"

Cody laughed, disturbingly unapologetic. "We know good work when we see it. It's not supposed to be a personal insult."

Across the room, Rebecca and Todd waved good-bye and stepped toward the door, smiles wide. Carefree.

As they should be.

Piper's donation was part of ensuring that would continue. To think he'd been focused on how she'd keep up with inventory and driving, totally oblivious to this huge undertaking.

Graham forced a deep breath. "The bids on furniture could run in the thousands, so it's important. How's she going to refinish a whole bedroom set and who knows what else when she can't even walk?"

"She's going to need help."

"Not mine. I have no patience for people who can up and walk away." Or at least, he wished that were true. Since he'd interacted with Piper again, baffled helplessness had haunted him once more. He'd told himself she had ended their relationship because she didn't love him, but if so, why hadn't he seen signs of it sooner? Was there more to the story than her excuses about Bryce and danger and his conclusions about her lack of attachment?

Cody nodded slowly. "Then don't be someone who walks away. Nothing about you and Piper needs to change for you to come through on supporting the Rasinskis."

Graham scowled.

"Maybe you two can finally move past all this. Move on."

"What do you think I've been doing these last two years?"

"Hunkering down in a corner of bitterness."

Graham shook his head and laughed, but the memory of the comment he'd made about cooking—and her response about the cabinet—suggested they both still carried some unresolved ... feelings. If not bitterness, then at least defensiveness and hurt.

"That foot looked awfully tender at church on Sunday."

Graham had noticed too. She'd let out a little cry when she'd kicked one of her own crutches. He'd barely resisted the concerned circle that had formed around her. He deserved a medal for not stopping by Second Chances to ask what the specialist had said. Her health wasn't any of his business.

Cody tapped the poster. "Consider this a double opportunity. You can help a family in need and maybe get your chance at what you didn't get the last time someone suddenly fell through on you."

Graham's stomach hardened in leery expectation. Had he really said enough to Cody that his friend could make the connection between Piper and what happened decades before?

"Your mom disappeared with no explanations, no nothing." Cody eyed him, no hint of an apology in his voice. Apparently, Graham *had* shared enough. "You never got closure."

His parents divorced when he was nine. Mom never wanted custody. She preferred to breeze in and out for quick visits. For a couple of years, anyway, until she gave up on that too.

"Maybe you and Piper are over," Cody continued, "but I know you've got questions. With her, you can get answers. Especially if you hang around long enough to do all this." He tapped a finger next to the line about her donation.

Graham shook his head. If his friend wanted to motivate him, bringing up Mom was not the way to do it. "Not happening."

He stalked off, but the idea stalked him.

He didn't want to revive what he'd thought he and Piper had once enjoyed—how could he trust her not to bail again? Closure did hold appeal, but enough to go refinish a bunch of furniture for her?

No way.

Chapter Six

Graham parked under the glow of one of the few lights in the Second Chances parking lot. A few blocks from the square, the store was addressed to Main Street with a parking lot in back. Light shone through the glass door, where the sign remained flipped to "open."

Crisp air met him as he climbed from his truck. In another two weeks, Thanksgiving would kick off the holiday season. Still, it could be a while before the first real snowfall. Even then, the accumulation rarely amounted to more than a couple of inches and tended to melt quickly, making white Christmases more miss than hit.

Whatever happened here, he usually got to enjoy snowy mountain vistas on the drive to spend Christmas with his dad and siblings. They all still lived a few hours to the east where he'd grown up, near Denver. The year he'd taken Piper with him, he'd gotten just as much joy—maybe more, even—from listening to her contented sigh as she enjoyed the serene white landscape.

About a week after they'd returned to Redemption Ridge, he'd arrested her brother. A couple of weeks afterward, he'd proposed. His chest tightened at the memory, him kneeling in the middle of one of their favorite restaurants, her grimacing as she said, "You know I love you ..."

Until then, he'd thought she had. The pain and frustration swelled until he growled to vent some of it before he went in to face her.

"This is for the Rasinskis." A little more of the pressure ebbed. He took a few deep breaths, then pulled open the door to Second Chances.

"Sit." Piper's bright command came from farther inside.

He stepped around racks of clothes and a freshly painted dresser. The shop smelled of cinnamon, pine, and vanilla. The register sat on a long counter made of reclaimed wood. Only the loose pieces of hair flipping from Piper's clip stuck up over the worksurface until he neared. Her brown eyes appeared, then widened. "Graham."

Behind the counter, she'd fit a cart loaded with clothes next to her office chair. She wore a cozy sweater, and a walking boot stuck out from under her wide-leg jeans. Opposite the clothes she was sorting, haphazardly arranged boxes encircled Teddy. Piper's injured foot rested on one such box, and the puppy sat in the middle, waiting for a treat. Piper passed him one, then struggled to her feet. Or, rather, her foot.

He should've been thinking up something to say as he walked in, not dreaming of Christmases gone by. Now on the verge of asking if she could handle her donation, he realized how awkward this could be. What was the best, non-offensive way to ask if she'd bitten off more than she could chew?

Piper motioned to Teddy, who attempted to scale the crate of magazines between him and freedom. "He was tired after you left last week. I thought it might've been the training."

"Best way to wear out a puppy."

"I posted a picture of him on the store's social media

accounts. He's been drawing in customers who need that extra excuse to shop."

She'd turned one of her obstacles into a benefit, proving she could look out for herself, as he'd been telling himself all week. The doctor seemed to be looking out for her too. Instead of her crutches, a kneeling-style scooter stood nearby.

"You saw the specialist?"

"Yeah. Three breaks after all. I'll be in a boot until Christmas."

So maybe she couldn't overcome every obstacle. From his pocket, he pulled the spare flyer he'd collected from the station's front desk and straightened the paper for Piper to see. "Tell me this furniture is ready and waiting."

She fixed her focus on the counter, the pink of her cheeks deepening. "I have some of the pieces."

"How many?"

"Half." She held up one hand, the white crescents of her nails peaking over her fingertips.

Five was *half*? Each one represented hours of work. Piper only had two part-time employees to help run the store, one a high school student and the other a semi-retired grandmother. No way the three of them could manage the shop and the donation.

"And those first five are ready to go?"

She bit her lips together in a silent no. "But look. It's not your problem, and honestly, Bryce ... I don't know. Maybe I was wrong to sign him up for your team."

The confession within the statement hit so hard, his head tipped forward. "You signed him up for my team on purpose?"

Her face blanched.

"Why?"

"Well, until I saw you two interact on Friday, I was hoping ..." She fiddled with the sleeve of her sweater. "He's angry and acting out. The Cakery debacle was one episode in a much longer pattern, and I don't know what else to try. The stuff with his dad is the root of his behavior, and since he blames you for the arrest, I thought seeing you in a different light might help him resolve some things."

He stared. "One of the reasons you ended our relationship was because he hates me. I offered then and there to earn his trust, and you shut me down cold. Now you orchestrate this?"

"I didn't know what else to try."

"How about picking up a phone and saying, 'Hey, Graham, I was wrong about you and Bryce. Think you can mentor him?'"

"And would you have?"

"Yes."

She frowned skeptically, about to question his character, no doubt.

"No. Don't. This whole—" He cut himself off and clenched a fist in front of his mouth.

Signing Bryce up for his team on purpose while making the arrangement sound accidental went to prove Piper wasn't always forthcoming. The deceit added to his theory that she hadn't been honest about their split either. But suspecting her side-stepping the truth and voicing the accusation were two different things.

A little bark sounded—and not from behind the counter.

"Oh no." She leaned over the boxes and crates meant to contain the puppy, scanning all directions. In frustration, she thumped her hands against the barrier. "I guess all these are good for is keeping me in."

So much the better. The anger zapping through his veins would only result in regrets if he didn't take a step back. He set off between clothes racks, around a display table, and to a fitting room. There, he found Teddy pouncing on a slip of receipt paper.

He carried the rascal back to Piper. "Where do you want him?"

"I should've borrowed a baby play pen for this." The strain in her voice played on his sympathy. She was overwhelmed, and considering the furniture donation on top of everything else, he couldn't blame her. Even without an injury, she'd over-committed.

Their breakup still ached like a broken bone. Truth might set them both on the path to healing. Or it might make him even angrier.

Thinking more clearly would be easier without Piper peering up at him with those wide, overwhelmed eyes.

He passed the dog to her. "I'll see what I can find in the storeroom."

Chapter Seven

Piper struggled to settle the squirming puppy on her lap. Perhaps the difficulty resulted from her own desire to squirm as Graham disappeared into the stockroom. She should've been upfront about her reasons for signing Bryce up for basketball—and about the little phone call she'd made to ensure he landed on Graham's team. Letting her ex in on it from the start would've shown more respect.

And she did respect him. Really.

She respected him so much that even now, she believed he'd set aside his feelings about her—well-deserved feelings—and do his best for Bryce. He was nothing if not self-sacrificial. If only he didn't resent her for the one time she'd refused to accept his sacrifice.

Of course, he didn't know that was what she'd done. If he did ever find out, he'd argue the choice hadn't been hers to make, but Graham spent so much time looking out for others, it'd been high time someone else looked out for him. And so, though it'd broken her heart as much as it'd angered his, Piper had done it.

She would smooth things over as best she could when he got back out here.

But he sure took a long time in the stockroom. Since the puppy wouldn't settle down for a nap, Piper set him on the floor and resumed practicing *sit* and *down*.

A customer came and went, but still no Graham. A pair of women entered and began a slow tour of the shop, focusing on the home goods. The decorative pillows a local gal made had been going fast, and one of the ladies tucked one under her arm. The other chose a few skeins of yarn Piper sourced through Bertie's Alpaca Farm, the business sponsoring Bryce's basketball team this year.

Still no sign of movement from the stockroom, although she could hear the occasional ripping noise. What was Graham doing?

The pair of shoppers had reached the back of the store when he emerged. He edged around them with large pieces of cardboard duct taped together. At the end of the checkout counter, he unfolded it, revealing a waist-high rectangle big enough for Teddy to move around in. He stepped close to pick up the dog.

"I'm sorry I didn't tell you my plan from the start."

Graham straightened, his hair rumpled from the work he'd done, Teddy against his chest. The pair of them made an irresistible combination of ruggedly handsome and downright adorable. "I want to help with the auction furniture."

"You what?" She'd assumed she'd blown her chance at that.

He nodded once.

"Why?" she asked.

He watched her and ignored Teddy, even as the puppy started licking his hand with fervor. The corner of his mouth twitched. "Tell me why we broke up, and I'll tell you why I'm helping."

Her pulse kicked up. If he was offering help because of some twisted fantasy about getting back together, she needed to put an end to it. But the whole truth about their breakup? That was the one thing she couldn't explain. "Your job is dangerous."

The partial truth didn't explain everything, but she prayed it would explain enough.

He shook his head once. "You knew from day one what my job was. Try again."

She rubbed her tongue against the roof of her mouth, but she couldn't spit out the rest of the story. What she knew best about family was how easy it was to lose. She'd never wanted to subject herself or anyone else to such deep pain, and she had no excuse for letting her guard down long enough to fall for Graham—and, worse, to allow him to fall for her. He wanted kids. She'd barely tolerated the risk of loving one person, let alone a whole family.

"The only change was that I arrested your brother," he supplied.

"That was for the best. In prison, he got clean. He's involved with a ministry, is a new person. But your job ..." She swallowed, checking what she was about to say. It would be true, even if there was more to it. "I'm glad there are people out there brave enough to walk into danger instead of away from it, but I can't tolerate that much risk."

Granted, *any* risk was more than she could tolerate, but that was hard to explain to people. They called her a pessimist. They thought her too fearful. They argued she ought to have more faith.

And maybe she should. But she'd seen so many bad things happen that she'd learned to expect more around every turn. In fact, the only reason she and Graham had reconnected at all after two years of silence was yet another accident.

"Why did you answer my text?" she asked.

His throat pulsed with a swallow. "I was concerned."

"Concerned enough to come check up on me, despite everything."

His gaze traveled her face like he was scanning puzzle pieces, looking for the complete picture.

"I bet it didn't feel good," she said.

His look of concentration neared a scowl.

"Concern, worry, fear. None of it feels good. And you didn't have to be in an accident for me to feel those things. Every time you were on the clock and I heard about something happening, I worried. What if you were involved? What if you were in danger?" She bit her lip, rising emotion warning her off continuing.

Graham's inhale sounded like a precursor to a rebuttal, but Teddy sank his teeth into his hand. He hissed and set the dog in the new pen. As he straightened to his full height, the shoppers appeared next to him, ready for checkout. The left side of her face heated as she rang up their sales because she could feel Graham's attention fixed on her from that direction.

She managed to keep her gaze averted as the ladies accepted their bagged purchases. She bid them as cheery of a farewell as she could, knowing Graham was waiting to finish their conversation.

Maybe something else would catch their eye on the way out.

But no. Because God never orchestrated such details when Piper needed them.

Flustered and desperate for a place to hide, she turned toward the pile of clothes next to her behind the register. One of her regulars had dropped them off today, and she needed to decide which to buy and which to pass up.

"That's the real reason?" he asked. "You *really* couldn't tolerate my job?"

"You'd never be happy with me, Graham."

"Why not?"

Because he wanted kids, and she couldn't set herself or the next generation up for the possibility of so much loss. She couldn't give him the family he wanted. He'd said it was okay if she never wanted kids, but then he'd made occasional remarks that suggested his desire for them hadn't ebbed. Remarks like the one he'd made at her house the other day, about people getting married because they wanted love and a family.

She couldn't allow him to sacrifice that dream for her. She wanted him to live a happy life full of all the love he could find, and she begged the Lord that if and when he did, he'd get to keep it.

Graham crossed his arms. "That's a no on baring our hearts and sharing our deepest motivations, then?"

Apparently, although she highly doubted his reasons for refinishing furniture went as deep as her reasons for saying no when he'd taken a knee. They'd been broken up for years. This shouldn't be an issue anymore. There was no harm in accepting his help and getting on with life, right? Because there was no getting around how much she needed the assistance, and no one else had offered.

Everyone was so busy this time of year. In Redemption Ridge, the community pulled together for good causes. Fundraisers and events packed the calendar, especially around Christmastime. Between the barn dance, the charity concert, the Christmas choir, the cookie decorating contest, the breakfast fundraiser ... Her mind shorted out there, but those events only scratched the surface. With so much going on, who could spare enough time to complete the donation for the Rasinskis?

Graham would be a lifesaver in one way and a major risk in another.

"It's supposed to be Second Chances furniture." Her voice sounded weak, almost hoarse. She cleared her throat to sound less like she was grabbing any excuse she could find to send him away. "I can't hand it over to someone else. The store's on the flyer." Movement caught her eye. Teddy prowled the perimeter of his pen.

"I'm the one who taught you to refinish furniture in the first place. I'll refinish it here, where you can supervise. I don't have the space at my place anyway. I can come before or after my shift, depending on when I'm on duty."

"You won't be home much. What about your dog?"

"Daycare. He loves it there."

The man had an answer for everything—except the one question she really wanted him to tackle: Why help her? She studied him, wishing he had ever worn his thoughts on his face. "I just need to be sure this isn't an attempt to get back together."

He laughed ruefully. "Believe it or not, I'm not interested in more pain."

"Something we agree on."

He gave a humorless smile. "Since I know how bad it feels to wonder, my real reason is the Rasinskis. They're good people."

She let the poorly-concealed jab slide. "Okay. That's how I feel too, so we agree on two things."

"Great." Graham's focus dropped to Teddy, who stretched his paws toward the register. "I'll start tomorrow. Want me to take him out before I go for the night?"

"That'd be great." She lifted Teddy's leash from behind the counter.

Great, great, great. Except, none of this felt great. It felt like opening the door to heartbreak and asking it to set up shop in the stockroom.

He accepted the nylon lead, his fingers brushing hers.

She pulled her hand back as a zing ran up her arm. Graham wasn't the only one who needed a warning that she wasn't looking for romance. Her own hand was out to betray her.

Chapter Eight

"She insists it was the danger of the job." Graham's black coffee tasted nowhere near as bitter as the statement. He finished off his mug and set it on the table at Flapjacks, an all-day breakfast restaurant. Out the windows overlooking the town square, Redemption Ridge was coming to life with slanting morning sunlight and increased traffic.

Cody wobbled his head as he chewed a mouthful of omelet. He gulped and followed up with a long drink of milk. "Didn't Casper and her boyfriend break up for the same reason?"

Officer Neenah Casper had only been on the force for two years. Graham hadn't spent much time with her, but he had heard she'd suffered a breakup right around the time he and Piper had split. "That was different."

"How so?"

"I wasn't a twenty-three-year-old rookie breaking up bar fights between men twice my size." Not that Casper couldn't handle herself. A former rodeo trick rider, the woman had strength, courage, and discipline in spades. At this point, she was a twenty-five-year-old officer with a promising career ahead of her.

Cody used the edge of his fork to cut another bite from his omelet, cheddar and ham oozing out. "You sure Winston Smalls isn't twice your size?"

The regular offender was pretty hefty. Thankfully, the guy was more bluster than bite.

"I have over a decade of experience." He watched Cody wolf down more food. His own meal had come with a side of bacon, but he'd filled up on eggs and toast. He nudged the smaller dish toward his friend. "So you can be twice my size too."

Cody snorted and snatched up the offering. Between his metabolism and his workout regimen, it'd take more than a couple of slices of bacon for him to pack on pounds. "It's not unprecedented, people not wanting to be with a cop. Why don't you believe her?"

"Because when I asked if that was the real reason, she froze up."

Cody smirked. "Why do they keep passing you over for detective with those observational skills?"

Graham didn't bother defending himself. After obtaining his degree in criminal justice, he had worked in the Denver area for the first five years of his career. Weary of the continuous onslaught of serious crime in a larger city, he'd moved to Redemption Ridge five years ago. He was a lot happier here, where he could make an impact, not only by dealing with crimes as they came up, but by developing relationships with the residents.

The local criminal investigators must've also been very happy within the Redemption Ridge Police Department, because only a handful of detective positions had opened up since Graham's arrival. Then again, it was a small department, and he'd known moving to the small town would limit advancement opportunities. When the Lord willed it, he'd get the promotion. With it would come regular hours and less walking into dangerous situations on the street, which might allay Piper's concerns.

Except he didn't plan to get back together with her, so why would that matter?

Bella Knight, whose father owned the restaurant, appeared beside the table. "Can I get you anything else?"

"More bacon, maybe?" Graham asked Cody.

"No, thanks." Cody chuckled. "The checks, please."

"I thought that might be the case." The petite blond pulled the slips from her apron and laid them facedown on the table. "No rush. You two take care." She slipped away to tend to the next table.

"So you're sticking close to learn Piper's real reasons?" Cody started on the last piece of bacon.

"Nope. I'm pitching in for a family who needs the extra support."

Cody took a drink and went back to his omelet, but he kept eyeing Graham.

"What?"

"You're trying awfully hard to get an explanation for a guy who isn't interested in it."

"I do want to know. It's just not my main reason."

Cody assessed him a moment longer, but instead of pressing, he checked his watch. "Duty calls." He drained the rest of his milk and scooted to the edge of the booth.

They settled their bill and went their separate ways, Cody to the station and Graham to Second Chances. The sign on the back door was turned to closed, with the posted hours promising the store would open in an hour and a half. Graham reached for his phone to text Piper to let him in, but then again, she might've left it unlocked for his arrival.

44

He tried the handle. Sure enough.

He found Piper in the stockroom, balanced between her tiptoes and the scooter as she reached for a box on top of a tall utility cabinet.

He stepped forward. "I've got it."

With a startled shudder, she twisted toward him. Her hand clapped to her breastbone, and her shoulders deflated with a relieved sigh.

"Sorry for startling you."

She wiped her face and shook her head. "Should've known you'd be punctual."

"You could keep the doors locked until business hours. I can text when I get here."

"Then I'd have to make another trip down the hall. I shouldn't be jumpy. It's not like Redemption Ridge is a hub of criminal activity."

He debated his options. While he didn't like how much she worried, not every resident of Redemption Ridge would pass up an unattended cash register. "You could give me a key until the furniture is ready."

"Oh." She frowned thoughtfully and nodded once. "Good idea. Then you can work when I'm not here at all."

"Perfect." Or at least, it should be. Why did her cheery tone as she found a way to avoid him sting? Cody's suggestion that he wanted closure sounded better than the alternative— that some small part of him might want the second chance Piper had asked about. No way he was that messed up. He was here for the Rasinskis. Plain and simple. Piper could avoid him all she wanted. "Where do you want me to start?"

She swung her hand through the air like she was washing a window between her and a collection of furniture in the corner. "Take your pick." She paid him the compliment of giving him a basic rundown of where to find tools without delving into how to clean up the pieces for their new paint.

She opened the utility cabinet and showed him the colors she'd chosen. "They all complement each other so the final display at the auction will look cohesive. Use the brighter colors, like the teal green, on smaller pieces. For the bedroom set and any other big stuff we collect, keep it neutral. Beige or gray."

"Aren't colors usually an important choice in stuff like this?"

"Oh. Well." She smiled toward the ragtag pile of furniture. "I trust you."

With paint, but not his skills on the job.

Smile fading, she raised a finger. "Don't even think of saying you didn't think I did."

"Wouldn't dream of it." He'd thought it. He hadn't planned on *saying it*.

She narrowed her eyes, lips pursed with a tightness that suggested she was hiding a smile. He used to love kissing those lips.

He coughed, rubbed his mouth, and turned toward the furniture. A nightstand had been stacked upside-down on a desk, conserving floor space. He moved the small piece to the tarp Piper already had spread. "I'll start small. It's been a while."

"I'll leave you to it." Piper and her scooter exited the room.

Graham resisted watching her go. Whether her concerns about his job were the full reason for their breakup or not, they were obviously an issue. Someone had to step up and serve the community the way he and his fellow officers did. If Piper couldn't understand that, it didn't matter what hare-brained ideas his heart latched onto. She wasn't the one for him.

If such a one even existed.

A power sander lay among other tools and hardware on a long table. He plugged it in, hit the button, and the sander roared to life in his hands. He pressed it to the worn surface of the nightstand. As he passed the tool back and forth across the tabletop, fresh wood revealed itself, ready for its second chance.

If only relationships cleaned up so well.

Chapter Nine

T he rear entrance jingled to announce Graham's latest exit with Teddy, then sounded again a minute later to herald someone entering. Piper glanced up from the hang tag she had been about to attach to a sweater.

Lucy, clad in work boots, jeans, and a dusty jacket, rounded a rack of dresses and hurried to the counter. Her long, dark hair spilled from under her cowboy hat. "I don't know how you could part with a pair that adorable by sending them outside."

Piper laughed and went back to using a tiny safety pin to secure the price tag. It'd been a couple of days since Graham set up shop in the stockroom. Everything had been going smoothly. He'd given her a wide berth at church, and around his shifts, he worked on furniture in the back while she busied herself in the storefront. They hardly interacted except when he checked on Teddy. And even then, he spent more time outside with the dog than inside.

"I really thought you were more mature than this." Piper had watched as Lucy carved out a name for herself in an occupation dominated by men. Plenty of ranchers had doubted willowy Lucy had what it took to care for animals ten times her own body weight. Only by working smarter and harder than her competitors had she built a name for herself. How much of that would be undone if people heard her drooling over a man?

Then again, Piper appreciated being the one Lucy didn't have to put on a show for. They'd hit it off in high school and had been fast friends ever since.

Lucy grinned. "I said a very mature hello outside, for your information. But you owe me the scoop. What's going on here?"

"Nothing. His job's dangerous, and as far as I can tell, I'm one of his least favorite people in the world. This is for the community. Not us." She set the sweater aside and picked up a fresh tag for the next shirt in her pile.

"You have to admit, he's cute."

Not after she'd spent the last few days trying to convince herself he wasn't—as if she'd once failed to notice his smoky eyes and broad shoulders. "Attractiveness isn't everything. He'd have to be indestructible to turn my head."

Lucy guffawed. "You and I are friends, but I'm not inde-structible."

Friends were different from husbands and from children. But Piper didn't argue that because she would be devastated if anything happened to Lucy. Thankfully, in all the years they'd been friends, Lucy had never broken a bone, had a fender-bender, or so much as slipped on the ice. She was close with her siblings and parents, ran a great veterinary practice, and had a lovely home. Maybe she was still hoping for Mr. Right, but Piper had no doubt God would soon provide him to round out Lucy's picture-perfect life. With all the cowboys, wranglers, and ranch owners she interacted with, how could she not eventually find love?

Anyway, compared with Graham, Lucy's life involved far less danger.

Then again, so did Piper's. And so had Piper's parents' lives.

What if something terrible did happen to Lucy?

"Oh no." Lucy raised a lecturing finger. "No, you don't. No worrying about things you can't control. We can trust God."

Easy for her to say. Piper pinned the price tag onto the shirt and moved on to the next piece of clothing. "Graham and I aren't getting close again. We're working together because he's the best option I have to get the furniture done while still managing the store. End of story."

With an unconvinced nod, Lucy turned her attention to the new arrivals near the checkout counter. "Speaking of things we can't control, Jack Carter needs surgery. He won't be able to go out on calls at all the week of Thanksgiving."

"Who's Jack Carter?"

"Another large animal vet. I was going to refer any emergencies to his practice on Black Friday and the day after so I could help here. Not only is that not an option, but he's referring his clients to me. Odds are, I'll be needed."

"Oh." Since the shop didn't do steep discounts, she'd estimated three people ought to be able to handle the post-Thanksgiving shopping rush. Piper and Ally made two. Karen had plans with her family, though, so Piper had recruited Lucy as the third person. Given her broken foot, Piper had been counting on the help, but animals in need of care trumped a bit of a wait at a register. Most locals wouldn't mind.

The bells in back rang. The tiny jingle of Teddy's tags advanced down the hallway as Piper pressed her lips into a reassuring smile. "We'll manage."

"Sorry." Lucy gave one more apologetic nod before returning her gaze to the rack she browsed.

Piper busied herself with price tags as Graham returned Teddy to his cardboard pen.

"What are you doing for Thanksgiving, Graham?" Lucy's question rose light and innocent. Too innocent. "Going home to see your family?"

Panic shuffled Piper's focus from Graham to Lucy and back again. What was her friend up to?

Graham scratched his cheek and avoided eye contact. "No, I have a shift that evening. It's too far to go."

"You'll be alone? That's too bad."

Piper braced for Lucy to try to foist Graham on her gathering with Bryce and her grandparents.

Instead, Lucy moved on. "Any big plans the next day? Going to hit up some Black Friday sales?" Her expression sparked with a little too much mischief for this to be a polite inquiry.

"This isn't necessary, Lucy." Piper tried to balance the warning in her tone with enough levity to keep Graham from suspecting what Lucy was building toward.

Uncertainty drew a line across his forehead. He knew something was going on, but for all his observational skills, he wasn't a mind reader. "I haven't seen any sales good enough to tempt me to face crowds like that."

"So you're free? Maybe you wouldn't mind working a shift or two here?"

Piper pricked her finger on a safety pin. "Lucy."

The poor man had just admitted he'd be alone on Thanksgiving, and Lucy wanted to add insult to injury with a Black Friday shift?

Her friend took a hanger off the rack and held up the blouse to block her face from Piper. As if the filmy fabric would block sound. "I was supposed to help, but I have to work. With her injuries and all, Piper's not up for Black Friday."

51

"I am. I'll be fine. Ally will be on."

Graham shifted, brows drawn. He shot Piper a pathetic look and gulped.

"I thought if you were going to be here anyway ..." Lucy lowered the shirt, far enough into this plea that she must imagine herself unstoppable. "Perhaps you could step in for me, since you two are getting along again?"

A tenuous ceasefire called for the greater good could hardly be called getting along. Piper licked her lips and focused on her best friend. "Ally and I can manage without you, Lucy. I don't need you to find a replacement."

Graham cleared his throat. "I planned to spend most of Friday working here before my shift. By the time I need to leave, I suppose business will be slowing back down again."

Was he saying he would help with the store in the morning? Piper closed her slackening jaw.

Triumphant, her friend slid the blouse back onto the rack. "Saturday will be busy too."

Graham rubbed his shoulder.

"That's too much to ask, Lucy."

"Why? You asked *me*, and it sounds like he was planning to be here regardless." Lucy fixed her gaze on Graham.

"As long as you don't have plans to open at the crack of dawn, I can help."

Lucy gave Graham a sweet smile loaded with hidden meaning. "I suppose she'll have to teach you to run the register and everything. I'll leave you to it." She waved her fingers at Piper, then made a break for it.

"Register?" Graham flinched as if the question physically pained him.

"No. I can sit behind the counter. I might need a little help with moving things around, but hopefully you can still focus on the furniture." She wouldn't have to be close to him, resisting the temptation to fall for him, if he was in back.

Chapter Ten

About ten yards from the bleachers, Bryce's blue-and-white basketball shoes halted with a squeak. Graham's lofty hopes of making a difference in the community—and specifically with Bryce—froze too. His heart sank when the boy pivoted back to collect his street shoes and jacket from the sidelines. His great-grandpa had already shaken hands with Kent and left, but if he hurried, Bryce might still catch up.

Each day when Graham showed up to work on furniture, Piper's smile grew less guarded, and he trusted he was that much closer to the explanations he craved. Unless he failed with Bryce.

"Wait." He jogged over to the boy as Bryce tugged on the gym bag containing his street shoes.

The strap had hooked on something under the bleacher.

"Where are you going, Bryce?"

"Home."

"You're quitting, just like that?"

Though his expression remained angry, Bryce's mouth curved down.

53

The boy hadn't liked it when Graham tried telling him Piper was counting on his help, so it probably wouldn't help to say the team was counting on him. But from the looks of it, Bryce didn't much like the idea of quitting.

"You must've gone out for the team for a reason. What was it?"

The frown deepened, and Bryce gave up on the gym bag. He swiped up his coat.

"Look. The way I see it, we can handle this like men."

Bryce's chin bunched, but he was slow about straightening the jacket to put it on. He was listening.

"I guarantee I'll make your game better. Coach Kent has got a lot of players to work with. My involvement means more individualized time for everyone, whether they're working with me or with him. If you did go out for the team for a reason, my being here will only help."

"We'll win?" Bryce forgot to look angry as he asked.

Win what? Games, or did Bryce have his sights set on a specific title? The stakes weren't exactly high for rec league basketball. "I don't know, but if you quit, you won't be with us if we do, and that would be a pretty awful feeling."

Disappointment weighed on Bryce's expression again, maybe at the idea of missing a winning season, but more likely at the idea of joining practice and tolerating Graham.

"I told you we could handle this like men." Graham took a step backward, drawing the boy's gaze. "Men don't have to be friends to get the job done."

He let that sink in for a moment, then turned his attention to his other players, praying Bryce would rejoin the group.

When he did five minutes later, the first thing Graham pictured wasn't imparting life lessons as a coach, but earning a smile from Piper for his efforts.

Chapter Eleven

Outside the window, autumn had been whitewashed by snow. Piper scanned the yard for a raised ledge to give an indication of how deep it was. Her scooter bumped the lower lip of the windowsill as she brought the patio table into view. The white fluff stood three inches tall on the glass surface.

Of course this would be the year when a significant snowfall came early. How would she manage a scooter *and* a shovel?

Teddy latched his teeth onto the hem of her jeans as if to tug her toward the back door.

"You don't know what you're in for." Although, with those thick curls of his, he'd probably barely feel the cold.

After pulling a winter boot over her good foot and a waterproof cover over the walking boot, she used a crutch to hobble down the back steps and let Teddy out. He barked at the snow, then dove headfirst into it. He tripped and hopped back up, white clumps clinging to his fur. If she'd brought her phone with her, she'd snap a picture to commemorate his first snowfall.

The scrape of a snow shovel against the sidewalk reached

her. One of the neighbors must be out clearing their property. Normally, Piper didn't mind the task. Hopefully, Bryce wouldn't, either, since she'd need his help. Today was a Monday, so he had school but not basketball practice, which should leave time to help out. Still, assigning him chores was a battle these days. Eking out as much of the task herself as possible sounded easiest.

As she fixed her coffee back inside, the house muffled the sound of shoveling. Maybe if she hobbled out there and offered to pay whichever of her neighbors it was, they'd take care of her property too. What was the going rate for snow-clearing?

She kept Teddy on his leash to better supervise him and carried her steaming coffee into the living room. When Bryce had returned from his first basketball practice on Thursday, he'd dropped the small duffle bag containing his basketball shoes in a corner. She'd asked him to pick it up over the week-end, but he hadn't, and she'd stopped noticing it. Now, on Monday, here it remained.

"Bryce, what have I told you about leaving things where they don't belong?"

"Um …" His feet plodded on the stairs. "Don't?"

"Run this upstairs quick. Mrs. Snowden will be here any minute." The family had been a true blessing, giving Bryce a ride to school and basketball practice. After his activities were done, Grandma and Grandpa had been picking him up and keeping him until Piper finished at Second Chances. Then, they'd swung by the shop with him to drive them both home. She hated to put them out, but they insisted it was no trouble, and this would only be short-term.

Much like Graham assisting with the furniture. Warmth and regret swirled in her chest.

Bryce gathered his belongings and took the first step back toward the stairs.

"Oh. Did they send anything home with you that I need to see? Any papers?"

The boy plunged his hand into the duffle and produced a green sheet. She'd barely closed her fingers on it when he thundered up the stairs to his room.

The informational paper outlined team fundraising plans.

Another to-do item for her list.

Outside, the sound of shoveling grew crisp, almost as if whoever it was had ventured onto her property. Perhaps a neighbor had taken pity on her without her having to ask? Redemption Ridge really was a great place to live.

As Bryce returned and pulled on his coat, Teddy happily tagged along with Piper to the front window. The Snowden's minivan eased up along the curb behind a large, black pickup truck.

A truck she recognized.

The truck that had given her a ride home from the clinic the day of the accident.

Teddy curled up on a nearby rug as Piper leaned to see out a window that looked on the driveway. Graham wouldn't be here, clearing the snow for her.

There was no reason he'd do that.

A honk reminded her Graham's truck wasn't the only vehicle out there. "Bryce, your ride's here."

He hustled up to the front, ruffled a startled Teddy's fur, then exited with a slam of the door. Thankfully, he hurried through the snow blanketing the yard instead of giving a second glance to the man who'd come into view in the driveway, pushing a shovel.

Graham lifted a hand in greeting. He'd spotted her, and wow, he looked ... handsome, healthy, and happy, his curls ruffled by the breeze, his cheeks pink from the cold, a blazing smile crinkling his eyes.

This was not good.

Not good at all.

The man was unreasonably attractive and loyal. Helpful. Way too easy to fall for against her better judgment. Love and a family in a world where God offered no guarantees of happily ever after was too risky. Especially for a woman who couldn't even navigate a parking lot without meeting trouble.

And even worse than her own crush, what feelings had inspired him to come help her? She worried her lip as he returned to his task.

Grandma and Lucy would heartily endorse the idea that he was falling for her. But they weren't exactly unbiased observers. Grandpa, however, was the most reasonable man to walk the earth—at least, in Piper's vicinity. A retired fruit farmer, the man believed in hard work, dedication, and facts. The fact was, she couldn't know how Graham felt. Another relevant fact? Graham made a living from serving the community.

Can't a man shovel a sidewalk anymore? Grandpa would ask.

Or at least, she imagined he might.

Chuckling, she left her post at the door and returned to the living room with the paper from Bryce. She lifted Teddy onto the cushion next to her and tried to focus on the team's fundraising plans. Teddy cooperated, curling into a small ball beside her. Her attention, however, kept drifting out to the driveway.

What if Graham *did* want a second chance?

He'd sworn he didn't. The simmering resentment in his eyes as he'd said it had convinced her. Surely, hanging out in the stockroom for a few hours wouldn't have changed his goals.

She forced her mind to the paper in hand. For the first fundraiser, the team would sell candy bars. She could easily support the effort. She'd put a box in her store and call some of the other small businesses to ask them to do the same.

The second initiative was a bake sale. She wasn't an awful cook, but baking wasn't her favorite thing to do, especially when it meant moving around the kitchen with a broken foot.

But she knew a great cook.

He was out in the driveway.

She gulped and vanquished thoughts of risotto and her imagination's line of inquiry about what kind of treats Graham might be capable of baking.

She would volunteer to man the sale, rather than offer to provide goodies. She didn't need to owe Graham Lockhart a single extra thing. Especially not if he'd try to collect on the debt by asking for her heart.

Chapter Twelve

G raham finished clearing Piper's driveway and returned the shovel to the bed of his truck. He'd put off deciding on his next move, but the time had come.

Should he offer to drive Piper to the store or leave her to fend for herself?

Someone had to drive her. Might as well be someone who was going to the same place at roughly the same time, instead of whoever she'd lined up for a ride.

He headed up the drive toward the front walk.

He'd already dropped his lab, Banjo, at daycare yet again. He missed the quiet moments around the house, just him and his trusty companion, but the dog loved daycare, and Graham's extra responsibilities wouldn't last forever.

Unless he kept adding to them the way he'd done this morning by coming here. His truck waited at the curb like a lifeboat. He could still make a break for it without offering a ride, but again, it wasn't as if this would take him extra time. He rang the bell.

Through the front window, he watched as Piper rolled up to the door, head cocked at a curious angle. She had to shuffle forward and back a bit to get close enough to turn the knob and swing open the interior door without hitting the scooter. Teddy stuck his nose through the opening first. Piper pulled her open-front sweatshirt, a cozy oversized thing, closer around her as he met them partway by pulling open the glass storm door.

"Need a ride to the store? I'm headed that way next."

"Why?" She already knew he worked nights this week and planned to go to Second Chances in the morning. She must be asking what work he hoped to get done.

"I'm putting the last coat of paint on the nightstand. If I hurry, I might be able to finish sanding the dresser. Best case scenario, I get to prime it too."

"No, like, why ..." She rolled her lips together and focused beyond him.

"Why did I shovel?"

"Yeah." She drew her gaze in, worry lurking in her brown eyes.

"Because it snowed." Each word felt like a step onto ice that might not hold. But where had this lake of resentment come from? "Is that okay?"

"Did you shovel for anyone else? Some of the shut-ins from church, maybe?"

"You realize you're one of the shut-ins from church until your foot heals."

"You shouldn't have come here."

This was crazy, having to defend himself for doing a good deed. "It only took fifteen minutes. I had the time."

She shook her head. "Still. You're doing too much for me."

"If you mean the furniture, that's for the auction, not you. I'm going to the store, whether you ride along or not, so it'd be

61

a stretch to call that a favor. You've got me on shoveling, but even that could be considered a favor to all the kids who have to walk by on their way to school."

"It's for the children? That's your defense?"

He'd done it for Piper, pure and simple. Injuries like hers hurt a lot less without strenuous activity, and he didn't want her to be in pain. "I need a defense to shovel a sidewalk?"

"Yes." Color crept onto her cheeks. "I told you, I need to be sure you're not bidding on a second chance."

Was he? Undecided. No. Decided. He was not. Or ... He pushed away memories—recent ones—of how her smiles had warmed him. Instead, he went on the offense. "Who talks like that? Bidding on a second chance?"

"It's a play on the word bid, since we're getting ready for an auction." Her mouth moved, but the rest of her seemed frozen, possibly with embarrassment.

Since he'd come to prevent pain, he probably ought to rescue her, but she'd hit a little close to the truth. "You're suggesting I'm so proud of my shoveling skills, I'd use them to try to win you back?"

Her mouth angled with an exasperated frown. "Yes. Because you like me."

"I do?" He managed to sound unconvinced, but the effort strained his throat.

Her eyes widened, the exasperation growing toward frustration. "I don't know. You tell me. Why else are you here?"

"It seemed like the right thing to do. As did offering you a ride, but if you'd rather put someone else out, that's fine." He stepped from the stoop onto the walk.

"You can't like me." Piper's statement reached him stark and clear. "You shouldn't. It won't end well. It's too risky."

Too risky. She'd said that the night of their breakup too, and both times, it echoed something he'd been told two decades ago. What about him caused people to reject him with such vague, weak excuses?

"Message received." He gave an exaggerated salute she'd see, even from behind him, and threw any romantic ideas of reconciliation in a prison cell and locked away the key.

Chapter Thirteen

Had Piper been avoiding Graham, or had he been avoiding her? By the day after the shoveling incident, she suspected it was both. Yesterday, he had surprised her by not beating her to the shop. When he arrived, he'd gone straight into the back without detouring to see her at the front of the store.

Today had been a repeat of the same. At first, the hum of the sander had underscored the shop's pop and soft rock mix. He'd been much quieter for the last hour. Piper hadn't given him much direction, but the nightstand had turned out as well as if she'd done it herself. Made sense, since he'd taught her most of what she knew about making something old new again. Whatever quiet work he was doing now would probably contribute to an equally beautiful job on the next piece.

Meanwhile, she'd wheeled her scooter around, straightening inventory and working on her tablet behind the checkout counter. That last part was how she'd found a bed she wanted for the auction. Online pieces like this tended to go fast, so she'd need Graham to go pick it up today if she wanted it.

Was it really worth facing him?

She clicked to zoom in on the image. She *had* wanted a sleigh bedframe exactly like this one. She texted the number listed and quickly received confirmation that the bed was still available.

Time to talk to Graham. Piper scanned the shop. Jeannette and Denise browsed the racks, but the regulars wouldn't mind if she disappeared for a minute to ask him to pick up the bed.

She was being silly, hesitating. She needed the bedframe, and the errand was distinctly for the Rasinskis. Graham wouldn't mind.

I'll take it, she replied to the seller. *Let me see how quickly my guy can get there.*

My guy. As though Graham was nothing more than an employee. Maybe treating him that way would establish the boundaries they desperately needed.

She checked on Teddy in his cardboard playpen and then headed toward the back room.

Graham had a dresser flipped to hand-sand the grooves in the legs. He glanced up, spotted her, and straightened. He ran a hand over his shirt, sending up a puff of dust and hope.

She even liked sawdust when it was related to Graham. This was so bad.

His eyebrows lifted, silently asking why she'd come.

Right. She was on a mission. "I'd like to pay you for clearing my driveway yesterday. Does thirty dollars sound fair?"

He grunted and took the sandpaper back to the dresser leg. "Nope."

She tightened her fingers around the rubber grips on the scooter. "Thirty-five?" He'd been out there less than thirty minutes. Surely, the first offer had been generous? Although his big truck probably burned a lot of fuel.

"You're not paying me."

"I want to. It's only fair."

He rose to his full height. "Fair?"

The ice in his eyes triggered an involuntary swallow. "Is something wrong?"

He laughed ruefully and returned to work.

She may have offended him yesterday by projecting her own feelings onto him. Still, this reaction seemed a little extreme. "I'm paying you, unless I can find some other way to cheer you up."

"I don't need cheering."

"Tell that to your scowl."

He bared his teeth in a smile that would've reduced a child to tears. His usual smile brimmed with kindness and joy. The scary grimace confirmed something really had gone off course. Perhaps the problem had nothing to do with her at all.

"Does it have to do with work?"

He grunted again.

"Cody?" Men weren't famous for friend drama, but there was a first time for everything.

"Did you know one of the last times I talked to my mom, she said staying in touch was 'too hard?'" Though he aimed the gruff statement at the dresser, his accusatory tone hit the center of her chest. With his head bent toward his work, she couldn't read his expression.

Was he angry with her for what his mother had done? As far as she knew, they hadn't spoken in years. Had the woman gotten in touch more recently, stirring things up again? "You were a kid at the time, right?"

"For my thirteenth birthday, she took me to see a movie and let me drink so much soda I was sick the rest of the day. A month later, I called her about coming to see one of my games, and she said it was too hard for her."

Protectiveness welled inside her. She had heard this story

while they dated, but the repetition didn't take the edge off. She and Bryce struggled sometimes, but she couldn't imagine giving up on him, especially if he were inviting her to spend time with him. And he was her nephew, not her own son.

How those words must've cut Graham. She'd experienced the hurt of losing a parent, but he'd suffered an additional blow—his mom had *chosen* to sever the relationship. "I'm really sorry she did that. No child should be abandoned. Is there … Is there any way I can help?"

Her ideas, to listen or to send him on an errand that might distract him, might not help much, but he must have some reason for bringing this up.

He tossed the sandpaper onto the dresser and crossed his arms. "She said it was too hard and disappeared. And you keep saying it's too risky, but life *is* hard and risky. Relationships mean staying committed, despite the difficulties."

Exactly why she hadn't made a commitment, at least not one with a ring involved. Her heart pumped fast and ineffectively, the edges of her vision swimming. She hated that he felt the pain she could see in his tense posture, in the line between his brows. She hated more knowing she had been a part of it. And yet, pain had been unavoidable. That was why she'd refused his proposal in the first place. "What are you asking?"

Graham's jaw worked. "I'm not asking to get back together. But I do need closure. You said Bryce hates me, but that's not a true obstacle, or you wouldn't have put him on my team. You said my job was too dangerous, but you knew what I did for a living before we started dating. You mentioned your own clumsiness, but I don't follow how that could have any impact on us. I don't even think you're afraid of commitment. You stick by your family through thick and thin—you visit Ryan in prison, you're raising Bryce. So tell me. Why did you truly decide I'm too much of a risk?"

"Because you're right. I do believe in commitment. I stand

by my family—Grandma, Grandpa, Bryce, and Ryan. But I've lost people too, and I don't want to lose more. So romance? I don't have the capacity to deal with that pain when I can opt out."

"Losing me didn't cause you pain?"

"It did. If I were a hiker stuck under a boulder, I think I could cut off my arm to free myself, because that's what ending things with you felt like."

He grunted an angry laugh. "I was a boulder holding you back?"

Her cheeks smarted, and she still couldn't get enough air. "One of the worst troubles I can imagine is losing the man I love. But even worse, what if something happened to our kids? Or to us, after they were born, leaving them orphans?"

All the anger drained from his expression, replaced by shock. "Our kids?"

Oh. The last they'd discussed the possibility of marriage and children, she'd shut down any mention of having kids.

"I thought you didn't want children," he pressed.

"It's complicated."

He assessed her. "I didn't realize that at the time. I thought you just didn't feel called in that direction. I proposed to you anyway. I was willing to sacrifice that. For you."

She gripped the handlebars of her scooter for all she was worth. "Sort of, but I knew you still wanted them. It was too much for you to give up." Her voice was small and sad. "I couldn't let you."

"So you broke up with me, even though you wanted the same things as me, because you were afraid something bad might happen to kids that didn't even exist yet." Even as he put into words exactly what she'd done, his skeptical tone suggested he still didn't believe what he'd heard.

"The Bible says we'll have trouble in this world. Case in point." She motioned at her boot. "I'm a magnet for trouble.

And with your job, you're likely to be one too. The only way to keep you from surrendering such an important dream *and* to prevent my worst nightmare of losing more people I love was to end it."

The sternness returned. "You don't know how our lives together might've gone, but you guaranteed a sad ending by breaking it off. We might experience trouble, but God is good. Life isn't all doom and gloom unless that's what you make it."

The statement stole the air right out of her lungs, and her cheeks flashed hot. She'd spent the last two years believing their breakup had been for the best. What if it hadn't been?

No. Not possible.

"I'm sorry our breakup hurt, but there are worse things."

"Than cheating both of us out of years of happiness because of some shaky 'what if'? Keep telling yourself that."

This was getting nowhere. She shouldn't have pushed. Then again, he might've confronted her anyway.

"Let me guess. This doesn't leave you feeling much closure."

He exhaled through his nose, lips curved in on a tight frown.

She'd wanted space between them and she'd gotten it. No going back. "For what it's worth—and I know it's not worth a lot—I'm sorry."

His jaw flexed. "Thanks."

She waited through a few breaths, wondering if she should try again to persuade him to see things her way. But what good would that do? If he finally agreed love came with too much risk, they'd still be forced to go their separate ways. "There's a bedframe for sale by Junction Springs. Since I can't drive ..."

Graham checked his watch and nodded. "Sure. I can make it if I leave now."

She texted him the address and looked up as he dusted his hands over his clothes, sending more particles into the air. He read her message, then pulled on his jacket and felt for his keys. As he produced them from his pocket, Piper's window of opportunity narrowed. He'd leave, still angry.

"For the record, I realize you don't agree with my reasoning, but I hope you can at least understand the heart behind it. Maybe, even though we didn't work out, you can forgive me."

"Sure, Piper." He clenched his jaw.

"If what your mom said also still bothers you, maybe you still need to forgive her too."

"She told me in no uncertain terms to stop reaching out."

"You don't have to talk to her to forgive her."

The tendons in his jaw worked again. "True." Without elaborating, he exited, the chip on his shoulder no smaller than when she'd first come back here.

Chapter Fourteen

W hat a sad way to go through life. Graham twisted a fist around the steering wheel as he drove toward Junction Springs and the bedframe. The leather squawked in protest.

How could Piper really believe the occasional trial negated the joy of relationships? Yes, she'd lost her parents to a car accident on an icy highway. Yes, Ryan had made poor choices. And yes, she was accident prone. But life wasn't all drudgery. Blessings abounded in the beauty of creation, in the warmth of friendship and community, the ties of family, all of it bound together with the love of God.

Where had she gone so wrong that she couldn't see the good anymore?

Someone operating under her mindset shouldn't call him out for being unforgiving. Yet that's exactly what she'd done. The farther he got from Redemption Ridge, the more he had to admit her point. Jesus had made forgiveness a mandate, and he wanted to honor God. But he didn't know how to drop his bitterness toward his mother.

It was much easier to focus on Piper. She was the one he

saw regularly, the one who was apparently willing to engage with him on topics like these, the one he wanted to see freed. Not for his own sake. He didn't need her running around his heart with a butcher knife like her fears still clutched in her hands. But for her sake and for the next poor sap who fell for her, he'd like to prove to her that life could be full and happy, if she'd stop letting worry wall her off from love.

But, God, how can I disprove lies she's spent years believing?

* * *

After Graham left on the errand to buy the bed, Piper returned to the sales counter, where Jeannette waited with a few of the dressier shirts Piper had steered her toward when she'd come in.

"How did you know I'd like these?" The thrilled amazement in the regular's voice was one of the best parts of the job.

Piper began ringing up the purchase. "You've gravitated toward what this person brings in before, so I had a feeling. In fact, I bet you two would get along in person too."

Jeannette chuckled. "You ought to have a meet and greet for your customers. Of course, with how many of my clothes I get here, I don't know what I'd wear. Someone else would see me in something they used to own."

"No harm in that. People like to see things they've loved being loved by someone new." She hesitated. How would she feel if Graham were with someone new?

She could set him up with ...

The thought churned her stomach. Better let him take care of himself in that department.

She blinked and finally hit the button on the tablet to total the purchase. "Are you buying the clothes for anything special?"

"Mostly work, but I think I'll wear the lacey top to Thanksgiving. What are your plans?"

So much for not thinking about Graham, because the first thing the holiday reminded her of was Black Friday, when he'd be helping. "I'm celebrating with my grandparents and nephew."

"Family for me too." Jeannette summarized her plans, but Piper got stuck on the mention of family.

Despite wanting a family, Graham didn't live close to his dad, siblings, or nieces and nephews. That's why he went so far for Christmas and why he'd joined her for Thanksgiving the year they'd dated. Since he'd said he wasn't going home for Thanksgiving this year, did he plan to spend the day alone?

Bryce would object if she invited Graham to their celebration, but she did owe the man something after he'd cleared her driveway, and no one should have to spend a major holiday alone. Pastor had been encouraging them to invite others to their tables over the next month and a half.

Ugh.

No. Where was this silly sense of obligation coming from?

Bryce's feelings aside, she couldn't manage a polite conversation with Graham either.

She wouldn't turn the dinner table into a battlefield.

Graham shoved his hands deep in the pockets of his winter coat and tracked the yellow line of the tow strap from the back of Cody's truck to the front of his own.

Maybe Piper was right, and trouble was the one guarantee in life.

He sighed. Pessimism meant his foul mood was getting the best of him. He hadn't been hurt when his truck slid into the ditch, but if Piper found out about this, he'd never hear the end of it. After all, ice had caused this, like it'd caused her parents' accident. He wanted to encourage her toward a healthier mindset, not feed her worries.

"Piper can never know about this."

Cody snorted and saluted him before climbing into his cab. Graham got behind the wheel of his truck, and with the vehicles working in tandem, Graham's truck slowly emerged from the ditch.

The trip to get the bedframe had gone smoothly until just outside the Redemption Ridge town line. A deer had run out, forcing Graham to brake on an icy patch that sent him straight into the ditch.

Cody unhooked the tow strap and sauntered back to Graham's window. "Get a real truck next time." He thumped his hand on the windowsill. A smug smile lit his features.

"Funny." Their trucks were essentially the same—different makes, different engines, but similar tires, four-wheel-drive, similar horsepower. Graham shut the window.

Laughing, Cody returned to his own vehicle. Swearing the guy to secrecy didn't guarantee Piper wouldn't hear. Any number of townspeople who'd driven by might tell her, and Graham himself wouldn't lie about it, should the subject come up.

He prayed the Lord would prevent that. Cody might've laughed it off, but Piper certainly wouldn't.

Chapter Fifteen

Even the sight of Graham's truck was enough to turn Piper's stomach in cartwheels. She exhaled, willing her insides to settle down before Margie Buchanan caught on that this trip to the rec center to check in with Coach Kent carried far more weight than it should.

"I hear the high school team's good this year." Margie, a real estate agent who'd kindly made space between house showings to drive Piper across town, steered toward the entrance. "With Bryce starting so young, someday, he'll be the star of the team."

A weight lifted. She didn't often think of best-case scenarios. Bryce excelling at a sport was a nice thought.

Most of the town attended the high school games to cheer on the Trailblazers. Was that why Bryce had gone out for basketball? He liked the idea of one day being the center of the town's attention for an hour or two each week?

Margie pulled to a stop. "You're sure you don't need me to wait?"

"I'm sure." She'd already checked with the mom who was bringing Bryce home that she could hitch a ride too. Piper slid from the passenger's seat. Before Margie could get out to help, she hopped on her good foot to retrieve her scooter from the back. "Thanks for the lift." She pressed the button to shut the back door of the van and worked her way inside.

Squeaking tennis shoes and boys' voices meant she'd made it in time for the end of practice, which was good, because she'd come to make sure Bryce and Graham weren't at each other's throats. After all, if she couldn't get along with the man, what were the odds her nephew could? To preserve his interest in the sport, she might have to have him switched to a different team.

She struggled with the heavy wooden door between the hall and the gym. None of the boys seemed to notice as they ran drills. Across the gym, Graham took a step toward her to come help, but she and the scooter made it inside before he could follow through.

Bryce turned away, probably avoiding any chance of overly-affectionate-aunt behavior. She aimed for the first row of bleachers and took a seat near where Coach Kent stood with a clipboard, watching his players.

By the far basket, Graham took control of one of the basketballs and demonstrated a drill for his players. He'd talked about playing high school basketball back when they dated, and his skill must've stuck with him, because he moved with easy coordination.

"Hey, Piper. I thought you might drop by." As Kent spoke, Graham flashed her an uncertain look, as if he could tell from across the distance she'd been admiring him.

No. Not admiring. Watching. There was a difference.

She busied herself by pulling her scooter closer to the wooden bench. "You expected me?"

"Sure did." Kent eyed her, then Graham.

"Oh. No. I'm here about Bryce. Well ..." She licked her lips. "I'm here about both of them. Graham isn't Bryce's favorite person. I wanted to make sure they weren't clashing too badly."

Kent chuckled. "Still sizing each other up from opposite sides of the court."

"I'm surprised he didn't walk out as soon as he saw Graham."

"Pretty sure he thought about it, but Graham got him to come back. Anyway, Wells aren't quitters."

Bryce's opponent knocked the ball from his possession, and Bryce vied to get it back. Piper didn't like to quit either. Maybe Wells *weren't* quitters. Except ...

"Ryan *did* quit basketball, as I recall." As a local, Kent would recognize her brother's name.

"Not exactly."

She peered up at the coach. He was a few years older than her and Ryan. Though she'd known he'd place her brother's name, she hadn't expected him to have an opinion on the matter.

"I'll never forget the day Coach had to bench him from the state championship."

"Ryan? My brother?" They had to be thinking of different people. *Her* Ryan had quit the team when he'd started running with a different, rougher group of kids. "Ryan Wells."

He laughed good-naturedly. "I know."

Her mind sputtered through possibilities. "By then, you would've been in college."

"I'd always liked Coach Rosenthal, so I commuted back to work part-time as his assistant coach for the Trailblazers Ryan's senior year. We had a pretty good run, making it to state. Can't help but wonder if the 'Blazers would've won with Ryan's help. He wasn't the tallest guy, but he had a lot of natural talent. Like Bryce over there."

"I thought Ryan quit."

Kent shook his head. "One too many violations of the

player's code of conduct. Coach encouraged him to come along with the rest of the team, show his support, but he was angry. Not just about the team. Mad at the world, I guess, since your parents ..." Kent cleared his throat. "After he got benched, we didn't see him again. Not at practice or games, anyway."

She'd remembered arguments between Ryan and her grandparents but only now began to understand how their hearts must've broken as he lost opportunities. Sort of like she worried more and more about Bryce. What if she couldn't keep history from repeating itself?

Graham blew a whistle and told the boys they could pack up, ending practice. One of the kids stopped by him, and from their gestures, she guessed Graham was giving him extra advice. Meanwhile, Piper watched through tears as Bryce plodded toward the locker room.

He could not go in the same direction as Ryan. Not on her watch.

* * *

Graham watched Piper pop up from the sidelines and start across the gym at a gait that looked suspiciously like a march, despite the scooter. She was on a mission. Had she heard about the ditch and managed to turn it into a personal affront?

He forced his focus back to the athlete in front of him and gave him one more tip before the boy turned toward the step-swish noise of Piper coming in hot.

"See you, Coach Graham. Thanks." He jogged off to join his friends.

Kent lingered where Piper had left him, grinning like a fool.

Piper's expression was anything but happy, though. She looked ... stricken. "I don't want Bryce to end up in jail."

"Neither do I." He smiled, hoping to put her at ease. "But he's pretty young for that. Juvie, maybe ..."

The attempt at humor didn't reach her. "You should come to Thanksgiving at my grandparents' house with us."

A part of him—a part he distinctly remembered locking away not long ago—lunged at the chance. He tightened his grip on the whistle he used during practice. "How is that connected?"

"He's ... He's on a path, and maybe you can help redirect him."

Graham rubbed his hand through his hair. "I thought he hated me."

"He'd hate jail more."

Graham wasn't sure about that, but the determination on Piper's face told him not to argue. She wanted his help, but did he—and not only the self-destructive part he'd put behind bars—want to get more involved? "I'll think about it."

Chapter Sixteen

Graham had disassembled the bed into manageable pieces when he'd picked it up in Junction Springs. Because of his little foray into the ditch, he'd run out of time and hadn't been able to drop it off at the store before practice and work, but the day before Thanksgiving, he slid the headboard from the bed of his truck.

Piper held the door for him as he angled into Second Chances. "Oh. They didn't say online there was damage like this."

His gut tightened. The headboard had been undamaged when he'd picked it up. Something must've broken when he'd slid. He propped the piece against a wall in the back room.

Sure enough. A one-by-three-inch piece of the overlay had torn right off. He ran his thumb over it. Piper was kind to think the problem had originated with the previous owner when the exposed wood looked fresh. "I can patch it up. We're painting it anyway."

"He still should've told us. This will mean more work."

He might not want her to know about the ditch, but he also didn't want her calling the guy for a partial refund. He took a step back and found himself shoulder-to-shoulder with her. He cleared his throat. "I didn't see this when I picked it up, so it happened in the truck. Probably when I slid into a ditch."

"When you what?"

"There was a deer and a patch of ice. Cody towed me out, no harm done."

"Yesterday? And you didn't tell me?"

"Like I said, I'm fine. The truck is—the deer, even." He ran his thumb over the splintered finish. "And I can patch this up with a little filler, good as new."

"But you had to get towed out? You should've told me. Was it steep?" Her hand pressed against her chest, and he knew her heart was pounding away beneath her palm. "What if you'd flipped?"

He placed his hands on her shoulders, looked her in the eyes, and willed her to calm down. "I'm fine, and I'm going to stay that way."

"Don't make promises you can't keep." The whites of her eyes turned suspiciously pink. And all over concern for his safety? After everything? "No one can promise anything. That's what I've been trying to say. The things we love make us vulnerable." She shrugged her shoulders in a move that seemed geared toward creating distance.

He let his hands fall away from her shoulders. He wouldn't force a connection she didn't want.

No. She wanted connection. He was almost sure.

She just didn't feel safe loving people. Maybe that's why her social circle was pretty bare bones—she was only close with a few immediate family members, Lucy, and, recently, him. Even if they would never build a future together, he did have an opportunity almost no one else had to speak into her life.

"Okay. You're right. I can't make promises about what'll

happen in the future, but I am fine, and I trust God with whatever comes my way."

"Anyway ..." She hoisted a plastic smile. The tears he'd predicted shimmered along her lower lashes. Instead of changing the subject as it'd sounded like she was about to do, she executed a clumsy W-turn to point herself toward the stockroom exit. She was going to leave, toting all that fear and hopelessness with her.

"I'll come to Thanksgiving," he said.

She froze, her shoulders at an awkward angle as if she wanted to shrink into herself. As if hearing his offer physically pained her. But she was in pain no matter what he did, and he needed a way to help her. Thanksgiving would be his chance to chip away at his relationship with Bryce, and he might also find a way to help Piper heal too.

"What can I bring?" he persisted.

She lifted a hand to her face, wiping away tears, maybe. Or maybe stalling as she decided whether to reject his offer. "I'll check with Grandma on the menu." The concession was a victory for Graham, but her soft and sad delivery dampened the satisfaction.

She was so afraid. What if the Lord had brought them back together to face this? To shed some light and hope into her life?

"Piper, seriously." He paused, second-guessing himself. Why was he doing this? And was he really in a position to get through to her?

She shot a reluctant look back at him. Fear would be her enemy her entire life if she couldn't defeat it.

He had to keep trying. "Don't let fear and worry do this to you. You can trust God."

"Of course. He's in control." But her tone held none of the peace that usually accompanied such statements.

"And He's good."

Piper curled her lips in, pressing them together, as she nodded.

"He loves you. You know that, right?"

Another nod, this one accompanied by a sniffle.

He rounded the scooter to stand in front of her. "I know you've been through a lot, but your life has good too. Don't lose sight of it. Tomorrow is Thanksgiving. Maybe that's the key here. Focus on what you're grateful He's given you instead of the losses or what-ifs or the future." He watched for signs of her hope returning.

She blinked a tear onto her cheek and angled the handlebars of the scooter as if preparing to go around him. It was almost cute how she thought she could escape.

Graham sidestepped into the way. "Teddy's pretty cute, isn't he?"

She let out a little, rueful laugh. "When he sleeps."

Though he wanted to brush away the tear, the touch seemed more like the sort of thing a boyfriend might do. He settled for a hand on her arm, the sleeve of her sweater soft beneath his fingers. "And your store is pretty great. Most of the town agrees on that."

A little of the sadness left her expression.

"Bryce went out for basketball, and that will be really good for him."

The corner of her mouth edged up, and she lifted her eyes to meet his gaze. "And I don't know what you're bringing to dinner tomorrow, but whatever it is will be delicious, so that's something to look forward to."

He was part of the positive she'd named? His decision to leave their relationship in the past shouldn't be so easily shaken. But from what she'd said, fear was the only thing standing between them, and he didn't believe in letting fear call the shots.

She studied his face. Was that a glance at his lips?

The knit of her sweater shifted against his fingers as she wobbled back. "I bet Teddy's chewed his way out of his pen by now." She shuffled until her scooter pointed toward the main part of the store. Moments later, she was gone.

* * *

Graham and I don't work. Remind me why! Piper stabbed the text to Lucy into her phone.

Graham cared. It'd been all over his face in the back room just now. Her heart pumped like a train engine set to chug right off a cliff. What if he *more* than cared?

There was no use sending the message, since she knew what Lucy's answer would be: she didn't see a reason.

But there *were* reasons. Bryce might benefit from having Graham in his life as a mentor, sure, but not as an interim father figure. Having Piper was one thing—Bryce's mom had split shortly after he was born. But Bryce loved Ryan, and he'd resent anyone trying to fill his father's shoes.

Anyway, Graham wouldn't be a father figure unless Piper married him, and she couldn't. Not when she might build a life with him only for tragedy to take one or both of them. Or for him to come to resent her stand on children.

Graham needed to keep his focus on Bryce. Help Bryce. Help with the Rasinski benefit. But stay far, far away from Piper's already bruised heart.

Everyone had already suffered more than enough.

Graham exited the back room. Light from outside cut around his broad shoulders as he advanced out the back door. As he returned two minutes later, she noticed the cold draft. He must've propped the door open to carry in the rest of the bed. She ought to go help with the door like an adult. After all, Teddy was sleeping, not chewing his way through the cardboard, and it'd be nice if some of the heat stayed in the building.

She gulped and grappled with the scooter. Graham, on his way out to the parking lot, took in the sight of her, his features serious, blue eyes clouded with regret that hadn't been there moments ago. He hesitated as if he wanted to say something, then silently passed her.

He was a good guy. One of the best. And here they both were, getting their hopes up. Why had she agreed to let him help like this?

Maybe she wanted to be wrong. Wanted to believe she didn't need to live in fear of the other shoe dropping. She'd never stopped missing Graham. That was why she'd never deleted him from her phone. She'd taken small comfort from seeing his name right there, next to Grandma's and Grandpa's.

Grandma and Grandpa. She should've mentioned them when Graham instructed her to focus on her blessings.

He returned, carrying the side rails. She opened the door and let him inside. He was good for her, but only if she kept him at a distance.

She'd said goodbye to him two years ago and hadn't looked back since. Surely, she could last a couple more weeks until Christmas.

She'd ended up needing him, but that didn't mean she needed to end up loving him.

Chapter Seventeen

B ryce entered the front door of Second Chances, arms loaded with boxes of candy bars. Tyler Snowden's mom, Heather, followed him in with more cartons. Coach Greely had distributed the candy bars this afternoon, the day before Thanksgiving, and just in time for Piper and Bryce to deliver them to the stores that had agreed to help the team. Dropping them off now meant most of these would sell on Black Friday, kickstarting the team's fundraising efforts.

Ally fetched a cart, and she, Heather, and Bryce deposited the load of sweets on its shelves. Piper donned her coat.

"You've got it from here?" Heather held the door while Piper and Bryce trooped out to the sidewalk.

"Yes, thank you." Piper rested a hand on her nephew's shoulder. "Bryce here's going to push the cart. I'm just along for the ride."

"Okay. Have fun, you two." Heather waved and returned to her minivan.

Piper and Bryce started down the sidewalk, the cart bumping over the cracks. "When you talk to each of the shops, be sure you thank them for doing this, okay?"

"Okay." They neared the first corner, and Bryce started into the crosswalk.

Piper grabbed the cart, stopping him. "Watch the lights." She motioned to the traffic signal that had turned yellow. "Always make sure the walk sign is lit, and look for cars, even if it is."

Bryce hefted a sigh. "I know."

But he hadn't looked. At ten, he should know better, but they'd been at this long enough that Piper knew he was sensitive to correction. He'd remember what she'd said, and he'd shut down if she pushed for an apology.

She went back to the topic of the candy bars. "After you thank them, tell them we'll pick up the money in a couple of weeks, unless they call and ask us to come sooner or later, okay?"

"Mm-hm." Bryce's eyes followed a sporty car as it passed in front of them.

They navigated the intersection. The first store waited another half block ahead. This was as good of a time as any for the other topic she needed to discuss. "You know how Pastor has been saying we should invite people to our tables for the holidays? People who have no one to celebrate with?"

Bryce's shoulders shrugged under his winter coat. He stuck out his tongue in effort as he wiggled the cart over an uneven sidewalk crack.

"I invited one of your coaches to Thanksgiving. He doesn't have anyone else to spend time with."

His eyebrows drew together as he worked that one out. Since Kent and his family of five attended their church, that left Graham. Bryce huffed, a firm scowl taking root. "So you like him?"

A memory of how close he'd been in the stockroom earlier stole her breath. Her feelings for him were irrelevant. She'd never act on them. "He's a friend, and he had no one else to celebrate with. Plus, he's a really good cook. And he can give you some basketball pointers after we eat. Grandma and Grandpa still have a hoop on the garage."

"I don't want help from him." His eyes darted to the sign above one of the storefronts.

They'd reached JoJo's Scrapbooking and Yarn, their first stop.

"Okay, it was just an idea." Piper rolled her scooter past the window, which featured a giant ball of yarn and three-foot-long knitting needles. "He is your coach, after all."

Bryce skewed his mouth and waited silently while she situated herself to hold the door for him and the cart.

Inside, she took a breath of air scented by yarn and paper products. She didn't knit or crochet, but the cute pens and journals always tempted her. She glanced at the displays as they crossed to meet JoJo at the sales counter.

The tall woman was in her sixties. Her hair was pulled up high on her head, and her cardigan draped to mid-thigh. "Oh, the goodies have arrived. Hi, Bryce. Piper."

"Hi." Bryce stacked three of the boxes on the counter. "We'll be back for the money next month."

JoJo's amused smile meant she didn't take offense at Bryce's gruff manners, but Piper nudged his shoulder.

He glanced at the shop owner. "Thank you for helping my team."

"You're very welcome, Bryce." JoJo winked at Piper.

"Thanks, Jo. See you." Piper met Bryce at the door and once again used her scooter as a doorstop so he could maneuver the cart back outside.

They hadn't made it three steps before Bryce said, "I don't have to talk to him, right?"

"To Graham? You have to talk to him, because you must be polite. Understand?"

A horn honked, and Bryce looked to the street, but even

Piper couldn't pick out which vehicle had sounded the alarm or why.

"Understand?"

"Yes."

"Okay. And while we're at it, we're going to be extra nice to the shopkeepers today too. Make sure you smile and ask them how they are."

"How am I going to remember everything?"

"Focus on being nice. If you forget some of the other parts, I'll help you."

"Okay." He trudged on as if she'd asked him to do chores for each of the stores. Was he stressed about getting it all right or disappointed about Graham joining them for Thanksgiving?

She fit her arm around his shoulders. "You're a good kid, you know that? I'm proud of you for being willing to help your team like this." Because of the scooter, she couldn't manage the posture more than a few steps, so she released him again.

Bryce adjusted his shoulders as if to brush off the affection, but his lips showed the faintest hint of a smile.

She brightened her tone. "Okay. Let's have fun. And when we're done, what do you say we swing by Donut Haven?"

Chapter Eighteen

Graham didn't figure rice stuffing or mashed potatoes—even his version, which involved copious amounts of butter, cream cheese, and french onion dip—were the way to Bryce's heart, so he had made sugar cookies too. Using a turkey-shaped cookie cutter and some orange and brown sanding sugar, he had converted the traditional Christmas treat into a Thanksgiving dessert that was being passed around the table.

After Piper's grandparents, Ralph and Gertrude, took cookies, Piper placed one on her own plate and offered the platter to her nephew.

Bryce scowled at the offering. "May I be excused?"

Here Graham had thought he'd been doing great, sitting a couple of feet from Bryce and not having a thing go wrong. Bryce had even answered his questions about how school was going.

"You don't want a cookie?" Piper asked.

Bryce spared Graham a disapproving frown before answering. "I want to work on my truck."

"Okay. You're excused."

He disappeared around a corner. When he returned with a rattling box, he took a seat in the center of the carpet and produced a partially assembled vehicle. By the looks of it, belts and a motor would enable the truck to move when he finished.

Graham enjoyed sports and had a certain talent for cooking, but he wasn't a jack of all trades. Building blocks had been a brief phase, but he'd never taken an interest in the advanced sets. Still, he'd come to connect with Bryce, and if that meant building a truck, so be it. He pushed back from the table, gulped down the feeling of foreboding, and sat on the carpet across the pile of blocks from Bryce.

Bryce continued working silently. Graham angled his head to study the directions and the partially constructed truck. Because Bryce squinted at step thirteen, Graham began constructing the part detailed in step sixteen, which was constructed independently and then attached to the whole.

Bryce worked away, skipping step sixteen. Maybe there was hope for them yet.

When Bryce got to eighteen, he looked to Graham. "Done yet?"

Graham clicked one more thumb-sized black brick into place. "I think so." He passed it over to Bryce.

The boy tried it one direction and then another but didn't snap the piece into place. He leaned close to the directions, then studied the part. "This is backwards." He began disassembling the pieces.

"Backwards?" Graham grabbed the directions. He still didn't see the error, but the fault had most likely been his own. "I'm sorry."

Bryce was already clicking the blocks back into place in the correct configuration, moving with much quicker fingers than Graham. "I'll fix it."

"You're really good at this."

Bryce ignored him.

Graham sighed. Not wanting to dig a deeper hole, he retreated to the table, where Piper met him with a sympathetic smile.

She scanned the table, eyes brightening. "What's everyone grateful for?"

Gertrude and Ralph joined hands on the heavy ivory tablecloth. They'd dressed to match in cranberry-colored shirts and tan bottoms—a skirt for her, khakis for him—leaving little doubt about what they believed to be one of their biggest blessings.

Gertrude spoke first. "I'm grateful for another year with our family. For you, Piper, and for Bryce. We love you both so much, and every day together is precious." She smiled at her husband, passing the baton.

"We've got a roof over our heads, food on the table, and I still have the most beautiful wife in the world. What more could a man ask for?"

Gertrude beamed at her husband, and the two kissed.

Would Graham ever find a love like theirs? He wasn't crazy about the prospect of dressing to match, but there was little he wouldn't give for the rest of it. Come to think of it, if a cranberry button-down was the last obstacle between him and lifelong love, he'd get that shirt on faster than Piper could say *Happy Thanksgiving*.

Instead, her fear stood between them, as stubborn of an adversary as he'd ever faced on the police force or off.

Except ... for a moment in the stockroom yesterday, she hadn't looked afraid or disinterested. Even now, she looked happy. "A friend of mine recently reminded me how important it is to be grateful for things, so I jotted down a list."

A friend of hers? Him? If he was the reason for the paper she was unfolding, maybe there was hope for them yet. He rested his forearms against the edge of the table and folded his hands, watching as Piper studied her list, glanced at him, then refocused, her adorable blush setting in.

"I'm grateful for you two, of course." She laid her hand on her grandma's arm. "I'm thankful I wasn't hurt worse by that truck. A broken foot could've easily been the least of my problems. I'm grateful I have the means to be a part of the fundraiser for the Rasinski family. With a little help." Another glance at him. "I'm thankful for the many friends who've helped chauffeur me and Bryce around while I've been unable to drive, and"—her brown eyes rested on him without wavering—"for the few who have given so much more time and effort. I couldn't do this alone."

"We're always here for you, whatever you need, sweetheart." Gertrude put her arm around Piper's shoulders.

"I know." Piper held eye contact with Graham another beat, then leaned into her grandma's side hug.

And then everyone's eyes were on him. "I'm grateful I've gotten to reconnect with some old friends lately." He offered Ralph and Gertrude a smile, though as much as he liked the couple, he was most thankful for Piper. "And I'm helping with youth basketball. I'm grateful for the opportunity to make a difference with some kids."

A gagging noise rose from the living room. Bryce followed it up with a quick cough.

Such a cute kid. He stifled a sigh and prayed for patience and wisdom.

"What are you grateful for, Bryce?" Piper called.

"Coach Kent." Bryce stomped off. A few minutes later, he passed through again with a basketball in hand.

"Be careful of the street," Gertrude called.

"I know." The front door opened and shut, and then a basketball thudded against the garage.

Piper ventured to the front window and sat on the couch, eyes pointed toward the driveway, supervising.

"At least he's practicing of his own free will." Graham picked up a sugar cookie and carried the plate to Piper, who took one too. If Bryce wasn't going to enjoy all Graham's effort, at least they could.

Chapter Nineteen

"So." Grandma dipped her chin and pointed a look over her glasses to Piper.

She should've known that, as soon as all the males left the house, Grandma would have questions for her. Graham had gone to collect Teddy so she and Bryce could stay longer. Grandpa had pulled on a coat and gone to sit on the porch as Bryce continued to shoot hoops. Graham ought to return with her dog any minute, but that would be more than enough time for Grandma to fit in a good grilling.

She tried to head it off. "He's helping me get ready for the Rasinskis' benefit auction. I was overcommitted as it was, and then I got hurt."

"But this is Graham."

"Yes."

"Who asked you to marry him."

"Two years ago. A lot has changed."

"Like what?"

"Bryce. I have Bryce now."

If Grandma tipped her chin down any farther, she

wouldn't be able to see Piper. Which might be nice, considering the look she was giving her.

"This really isn't the time for a romance, Grandma. There's so much going on, and who knows what's going to go wrong next?"

"What makes you think something's about to go wrong?"

"I was hit by a truck."

"Yes, dear, and not many people can say that, but—"

"Not many people can say half the things I can say. How can I risk my heart when it's likely to get broken like everything else?"

Grandma chuckled. "But what if he doesn't break it? What if you take the risk and win a lifetime of wedded bliss?"

"It's not always a lifetime. There are a lot of factors, and plenty of them are out of anyone's control. Look at Mom and Dad. An accident cut everything short."

"They had a lifetime together. It was the length God chose rather than the one we would've picked for them, but they were happy together and happier still for loving you and Ryan."

"And now, if they were around, they'd be heartbroken at how it all turned out."

"Nothing's 'turned out' yet, dear. Nothing's done until we're safe in eternity with our Savior. When we look back from there, we'll understand what's incomprehensible right now." Grandma resettled her glasses on her nose. "You don't really wish they'd never started a family because of what might be."

She was right, of course. Piper couldn't wish she didn't exist.

"I think they'd be happy." Grandma patted Piper's knee. "Proud of you, and of Ryan for the changes he's making. They might long for more grandbabies, though."

"Grandma, please." Outside the picture window, Graham eased his truck along the curb. Another minute, and he'd be inside, cutting this short.

Grandbabies. Those were probably the whole reason for the interest in Piper's relationship with Graham. If being romantically involved with Graham opened up too many possibilities for disaster, children would bring even more. "Not everyone wants kids."

"True, but are you sure you're one of them? You were a doting mother to your dollies as a girl. And I overheard all the moms at church raving about your babysitting skills when you were a teen. You had a real passion for children. From what I can see, you still do." She tipped her head toward Bryce.

An image—or maybe it was more an emotion—flashed through her mind of what it would be like to have a family with Graham. But the fulfillment and safety that her brain conjured were nothing more than wishful thinking. Too often, life didn't work out like that.

If only the world worked differently. Would all the hardships really make sense when she was in heaven? Maybe. But surely God couldn't blame her for protecting herself a little bit in the meantime.

"Graham's a friend, and I'm hoping he'll be a mentor to Bryce. That's all." She watched him exit the driver's seat. Teddy, still in the cab, put his paws on the dash and peered out the windshield. Graham must have planned to get him out from the passenger side, maybe because the street was a fairly busy one.

Bryce threw the ball toward the basket, but it ricocheted off the rim and flew down the driveway, toward the street. He sprinted after it without checking for traffic.

Grandpa stood and called out as the ball bounced past the curb on a trajectory that would land directly in front of an oncoming car. Bryce didn't seem to hear the warning, and another vehicle advanced from the opposite direction.

Graham, the only one close enough to intervene, studied the other side of the street, completely unaware.

Chapter Twenty

That basketball sounded close. Graham swung his gaze from the huge turkey inflatable across the street and saw the top of Bryce's head over the tailgate of the truck. The kid was booking it. Graham had looked for traffic when he'd gotten out of his truck, so he knew how close the cars were without having to scan the area again.

"Bryce, no!"

The ball bounced into the first lane of traffic.

The boy didn't slow, but Graham made it into his path at the rear of the truck. Bryce slammed into him as tires squealed in the road. Graham locked the boy to his chest and rushed him to the sidewalk.

He bent to look into his wide eyes. "Are you okay?"

Bryce looked from Graham to the street.

A car door opened. "Trying to give me a heart attack? Look first, kid!"

Tears flooded Bryce's eyes, and he charged for the house.

Shaken but unhurt.

Thank you, Lord.

With a sigh, Graham turned to deal with the drivers, both

of whom had stopped, one with the basketball wedged under their front bumper.

Way too close for comfort.

As his adrenaline faded, the muscles of his back, arms, and chest felt every ounce of tension he hadn't had time for in the moment.

He verified that everyone in both vehicles was also all right and assured them Bryce was okay and that he'd talk to him about looking before entering the street. He retrieved the basketball, got Teddy from the cab of the truck, and started for the house.

Maybe this moment, as scary as it'd been, would mark a turning point. Bryce would have no choice but to thank him. Gratitude had transformed Piper. Maybe it'd do the same for her nephew.

* * *

"He had no right to do that! I was going to stop." Tears streaked Bryce's face as he slumped against the pillows of Grandma and Grandpa's guest bed. "And that other man had no right to yell at me. He should look where he's going."

Piper sat next to him, but since he seemed to think affection was for babies, she kept her hands to herself. "You didn't look, Bryce, and you weren't going to stop. You need to be more careful. You scared us all. We care about you so much. I don't know what I'd do if something happened to you."

"Nobody cares about me. Nobody but my dad."

Piper laid her hand on Bryce's shoe, desperate to make her point. "Your dad does care about you. He loves you very much. But other people do too. Grandma and Grandpa and I love you. And Graham cares, or he wouldn't have taken such a big risk, stepping in to keep you safe."

"It wasn't a risk. I *was* safe."

He hadn't been though. When Bryce slammed into Graham, Piper had thought Graham might tip backward under the weight, right into the path of the car. It'd all been so close that she hadn't even been sure Graham had escaped contact with the vehicle until he'd come around the truck, carrying Bryce in a sloppy but firm hold, his steps sure and even.

"Thank God for Graham," Grandma had said from beside her at the living room window.

"Amen." She'd thought she'd had a lot to be thankful for at the dinner table, but in that moment, she could've broken out into song over how relieved she was that Bryce was safe.

And Graham too.

Bryce had run into the house and allowed a hug before he'd started crying in earnest and retreated to the bedroom. His claims that he would've stopped on his own and hadn't been in any danger were probably his pride covering up his embarrassment.

Graham stuck his head in the room. "Everyone okay in here?"

Bryce harrumphed with gusto an old grinch would envy.

"You know better than to run out without looking." Graham spoke gently, but this was the police officer in him, unable to let the offense go unaddressed.

Piper couldn't blame him. The longer Bryce tried to blame others, the more she wanted to scold him into accepting responsibility. Enough bad things happened without careless- ness on the level Bryce had exhibited.

Graham continued. "If the ball goes in the street, it's just a ball. Always stop to look."

"It's your fault I didn't."

Graham drew his arms up and crossed them over his chest. "How so?"

"I was practicing my lay-ups. You distracted me."

"I see." Graham watched the pouting boy for a few beats. "You know, Bryce, in life, some things are so important that we can't let anything distract us." He looked at Piper and a pang ran through her core.

Was he saying she was important? Or only trying to make sure she was on board with his message to Bryce?

"Your safety is important," Graham continued. "You have a responsibility to take basic precautions. Nothing can prevent all bad things from happening, and we have to trust God when things go wrong, but basics like wearing seatbelts and looking both ways for traffic can prevent a lot of unnecessary pain."

Bryce didn't make eye contact with either of them, and so much the better, because when she checked, Graham's eyes were fixed back on her. Her plan to install Graham as a mentor to Bryce had overlooked an important flaw: He'd never been more attractive to her. Strong and kind, understanding and wise.

Graham fixed his line of sight back on Bryce. "Promise me you won't let anything distract you from something so important again."

"Fine. I'll ignore you next time."

Graham looked less than thrilled, but he didn't push further. Instead, he stepped into the hall. Piper patted the boy's leg, then silently followed Graham to the living room.

From the sounds of it, Grandma and Grandpa puttered around in the kitchen, probably taking care of the few dishes they hadn't all done together immediately following the meal.

"He's embarrassed, but I think he heard you."

"I hope so." Graham assessed her. "How about you? How are you doing?"

She shrugged. The turkey in her stomach still felt like it was doing jumping jacks. "I never want to see him in danger like that again, that's for sure."

"But you're glad I was there?" The edges of Graham's mouth lifted.

"Very. I just wish Bryce was glad for it. I want him to look up to you, but if he's always angry with you, I don't know how that'll happen."

"Give it time. We still have most of the basketball season ahead of us, but ..." He gave her an uncertain look again, then his line of sight wandered to the other side of the room, and he pushed his hand through his curls.

"But what?"

"But do you think you can believe what I said about taking the proper precautions and then trusting God with the rest?"

She stiffened as she suppressed the offense his question stirred up. "What other choice is there?"

"One option is to trust God with as little as possible by taking more than the reasonable precautions."

"Reasonable looks different to different people, I imagine."

He shrugged, but she sensed the careless movement hid strong convictions. "Seems to me one of your unreasonable precautions is that you stay single. You ruled me out because of my career, but I'm far from the only guy out there. Yet you can't bring yourself to trust God enough to date anyone at all, can you?"

She squirmed. In part, he was right. "Maybe no one's caught my eye."

"I have a hard time believing I'm that unique." But the way he focused on her said he hoped he might be.

He was. If he tried in earnest to resurrect their romance, she'd never muster the willpower to send him away.

She could not allow him to realize her weakness. "Okay. You win. I'll go on a date with someone."

Did he flinch? Hard to tell, the movement was so slight and quick. "Good."

She gulped. What had she just agreed to? And why again? "Why is this important to you?"

"Jesus offers freedom, and if you're bowing to fears, you're not living in it. It's hard to watch."

"You'd rather watch me date?"

"Yup." His answer came fast and firm, leaving little room for doubt. He truly wanted this, and that meant he didn't have feelings for her anymore.

She may have agreed to go on a meaningless date, and she had no idea how she'd find the guy to share an evening with, but relief flooded her.

She was safe. Her silly crush on Graham couldn't go anywhere because he didn't feel the same for her as she felt for him.

Chapter Twenty-One

Piper woke on Black Friday to her alarm, followed by the sound of hushed cartoons. Bryce must be up. She still had an hour to get to the store, where they'd already posted twenty-percent-off-everything signs.

It should be a good day. Her regulars would visit in a stream that would keep her from having to face Graham and all the confusion he stirred up in her. They'd both been clear they were not going to be an item again. But Piper also had no other prospects. She'd have to get Lucy to set up a blind date or something, because if she backed out of the date, Graham would either keep lecturing her about fear or, worse, guess how she felt about him.

As the coffee brewed, she stood in the door of the living room. Bryce sprawled on the floor, connecting more tiny building blocks. The TV served more as background noise than entertainment. Then a commercial came on with boys Bryce's age advertising a sale on a new building set. The colorful and boisterous commercial kept Bryce's attention rivetted to the screen.

Afterward, he switched his gaze from the TV to her. "Can

we get one? It's the space set. I don't have one of those yet, and it's only ten dollars."

After the funk he'd been in yesterday, she wanted to say yes, if only to build on the hopeful excitement in his eyes. Those building sets cost too much to purchase often, and the ten-dollar price tag would've tempted her even without Bryce's pleading look. But she had to work, and even if she didn't, she couldn't drive or navigate Black Friday crowds with a broken foot.

She'd asked so many friends for help already. This would be too much to ask.

Unless, of course, said person had already committed to doing a favor for her today.

"I have an idea, but you might not like it."

Bryce's lips jammed together in displeasure. He must've guessed her idea. A good experience with Graham might help him feel differently in the future. A trip to the store together would give them the chance to bond when she wasn't in the picture. Plus, it would keep Graham away from the store for an hour or two.

"I'd like to get you the set, but I can't take you."

Bryce returned to his work. "Forget it."

Piper upped the ante. "Three sets."

When her nephew's gaze lifted in interest, Piper hurried back to her bedroom for her phone to get Graham involved before Bryce could change his mind.

* * *

"At least we didn't have to drive in circles for twenty minutes to find a spot." Graham rested a hand on Bryce's shoulder as they hiked from their parking spot toward the store. One Wells getting sideswiped was one too many. He wasn't going to let Bryce out of reach until they were safely inside.

The kid glowered up at him, but Graham kept his hand in place. It was either that or hold the boy's hand, and he knew which would go over worse. They followed a trickle of others through the automatic doors and into the store. So far, he'd seen far fewer people than he'd expected.

The noise of overlapping conversations drew his attention left, toward the registers. There, a sea—no, an ocean—of people waited in line. Hopefully, Piper wouldn't need help at Second Chances this morning, because he and Bryce wouldn't get out of here before noon.

Why had he agreed to this?

Because when it came to Piper, the craziest things came out of his mouth. Things that encouraged her to date other men. Things like, *Sure, I'll take Bryce Black Friday shopping.*

Of the two, the shopping trip wasn't the worst.

His mental picture of her on the arm of some other guy blurred when it came to her companion, but he could imagine how she'd smile up at the man. His stomach soured.

"They're this way." Bryce took the lead and wove through the store like he'd done this often. He dodged a woman with an overfull cart and veered into the aisle of spaceships, cars, and building sets.

Graham gave the lady an apologetic nod as he waited for her to pass. In the aisle, Bryce's head bobbed as he looked at one half-empty shelf and another, searching for his prize. When he reached the end, he stopped and turned back, his expression wavering between disappointment and determination.

Heavy suspicion seeped into Graham's gut. He joined Bryce, reading labels on the shelves while the boy double-checked the boxes. Graham found the correct label beneath an empty space on the shelf. Not one of the sets they'd come for remained.

Bryce made it to the end of the aisle again and returned to stand at Graham's elbow. "They aren't here."

"Looks like they're sold out."

"But I just saw the commercial."

"I know, but it probably ran nationwide. They didn't know our store would sell out of them." He scanned the aisle for a way to redeem this. Other sets featured astronauts, even if the building blocks were larger, the design more simplistic. He lifted what he estimated to be the coolest of them. "What about one of these?"

"Those are for babies."

Graham put it back. "We can try online. On the bright side, we don't have to stand in the checkout line for an hour."

"But I wanted to build it today."

"I'm sorry." Graham rubbed his face and scanned the shelves again. He moved a couple of boxes in case one of the coveted sets had gotten mixed in, but to no avail. "I'll take you to your grandparents' house. At least you have a set there to work on."

Bryce scowled the whole way to his great-grandparents' house. When he climbed out of the truck, Graham expected a mouthy remark, but the boy slammed the door and headed away.

He watched until he made it inside and then pulled back onto the road, his own mood on the upswing. Next, he'd get to see Piper, and not even a herd of Black Friday shoppers could trample that good news.

Chapter Twenty-Two

Graham found more people inside Second Chances than he'd ever seen browsing the store at once. The dozen or so shoppers may mean Piper would need him for something other than furniture. He could handle a line of shoppers as long as he didn't have to stand in it.

Ally exited a dressing room, leaning backward to counterbalance a load of clothes. She looked about ready to tip over.

"You need help?"

"Nope. I've got it." She sidestepped to avoid a customer at the last moment, then pivoted toward the nearest rack of clothing to start restocking. "I think Piper could use you, though."

He squelched the grin that wanted to advertise how he felt about the suggestion. As he turned for the register and laid eyes on her, a sense of being exactly where he wanted to be settled over him.

Piper had maneuvered her scooter into the small space behind the counter and stood with her knee resting on it as she checked out customers. As soon as she finished with one, another got in line. The clip holding her hair had half let go, and the flush on her cheeks indicated she was either warm from working or flustered and stressed.

He touched her arm. "What do you need from me?"

"Graham." Relief washed over her face, and he committed the moment to memory. Her saying his name, obviously grateful to see him. "How'd it go?"

"Sold out."

Her shoulders rounded. "I hadn't even thought of that."

"I ordered from the website already so they couldn't sell out too."

"Oh. Great. I'll pay you back." She deftly checked out the next customer, her responses to the shopper on autopilot. She'd probably parroted the same few phrases three dozen times already this morning. As she began the next sale, she angled toward him. "We're having the same problem here, selling out of stuff. I need to get more inventory out of the back. Do you think you can take over checkout?"

"If restocking involves carrying things, I might be better at that."

"I'm afraid picking out which clothes to add to the racks is more nuanced."

"All right. I'll ring up sales, but you'd better walk me through a couple of transactions."

"Okay." Piper finished the one she was working on and handed the customer her shopping bag, then motioned him close enough to read the screen on the tablet she used to manage transactions. She explained details about tags and cash versus credit transactions in between answering customer questions and completing sales, but Graham could only half listen.

Her perfect fingers tapped the tablet screen. She had a whole system set up—because of course she did. It was part of running a successful small business. But all this reminded him of what he'd liked about her. She was dedicated. She had a way with people. She cared enough to figure out exactly what they wanted, even when they couldn't put it in words, like when one lady came up and started talking about how she was going to see her ex on Christmas Eve.

Piper pointed to a rack on the far wall. "There's a rust-red sweater over there. It's unbelievably soft and has the perfect neckline." She motioned over her own collarbone. If he read the movement correctly, the perfect neckline was a wide V. "Comfy as can be, classy enough for a church service, and pretty enough to give you that boost, you know?"

Apparently, the lady did know, because she zipped away to find the recommendation.

Without seeming to realize how amazing it was that she'd figured out what the customer wanted by the little she'd said, Piper dove back into his checkout lesson.

Had she ever made wardrobe choices based on whether she was going to see him? Maybe that was why she'd looked unbearably perfect after their breakup. Here he'd thought his longing simply stemmed from how out of reach she'd suddenly become.

Of course, there was never much fault to find in Piper's appearance, whether she'd considered him while choosing her outfits or not. She always looked pulled together. Usually in winter, that involved jeans and soft sweaters. The one she wore today was ivory, and when her sleeve brushed his forearm, his longing was back with a vengeance.

This was the sweetest kind of torture. Nevertheless, torture was torture. He'd told her to go on a date with someone else—*with someone else*—in a moment of believing the lie that he wanted to help her deal with her fears so she wouldn't break the next guy's heart.

He *hated* the thought of the next guy.

From here on out, he'd endure whatever torture came his way, but not another word out of his mouth was going to help the next guy. He was in this for himself and for Piper, and if he had his way, there'd be no next guy.

* * *

Piper could hardly breathe for how much space Graham took up behind the counter. The hints of spice in his cologne or aftershave—or whatever that was—blended with the shop's potpourri, rendering her every inhale as warm and sweet as a cup of mulled cider.

She fluffed her sweater away from her torso and told herself she wasn't overheating because of Graham. She shouldn't have chosen today for the thick material, even if it was cropped to the perfect length to pair with these jeans. All the customers and the fast pace really had her going. She fanned the sweater again, then finished checking out the customer who was in the show-him-he-lost-the-best-he-ever-had stage of her breakup.

Piper hadn't really needed that stage when she'd broken up with Graham. He hadn't wanted to lose her in the first place, and he'd never been the careless boyfriend her customer had complained about a few times over the last three months.

Maybe, in her own case, Piper had been the careless one, because she was having a definite moment of I-lost-the-best-I-ever-had. Graham had to be the best. If he wasn't, he wouldn't listen patiently as she fumbled through a million directions, half of which he probably didn't even need.

But the facts hadn't changed. Love came with risk. Besides, he wasn't even tempted by her. He wanted her to date someone else. And today's disappointment couldn't have inspired goodwill with Bryce. She needed to get out from behind this counter and to the back room, where clothes she hadn't yet ticketed waited for her. "Got it?"

Graham's brow furrowed, his gaze fixed on the screen of the tablet. "If something goes wrong, you won't be far."

True, but her hormones needed at least an hour of breathing less delectable air, or she couldn't guarantee what she might do. "I'll be in the back, but Ally knows how all of this works." She rolled her scooter, meaning to leave.

Graham stood in the way, still studying the tablet and muttering to himself. "Can't be any harder than directing traffic."

Piper looked at the tablet. Only four options showed on the first screen, but each one after featured another set of options. He might not be ready for this. Then again, even Redemption Ridge had a couple of busy streets. Maybe he'd be okay.

For the sake of her fickle heart, he'd better be. She rolled her scooter forward. "Excuse me."

"Oh. Sure. Sorry." He stepped out from behind the counter to let her escape, but she didn't make a clean getaway because a customer approached the counter, and Graham edged back in around her, brushing against her shoulder and back as they passed each other in the close quarters.

Her shoulder wouldn't have tingled more if he'd zapped her with a heavy dose of static. She scooted herself away without supervising his first transaction. He could give away merchandise for free for all she cared, as long as he didn't end up owning her heart.

Chapter Twenty-Three

Graham had to hand it to Piper; she knew how to dress for a basketball game. She'd probably only ever been to high school games before, where face paint was more common. At the fourth-grade level, Graham was just happy the parents had gotten the memo to show up at the high school gymnasium and not the rec center for the first game of the season. But if Piper felt out of place for having painted a "B" on one cheek and a stick-figure alpaca on the other, she didn't let it affect her clapping and encouragement.

"It's all right. It's all right. Next time!" she called when Bryce missed a shot.

She might dream up worst-case scenarios in other circumstances, but here, she looked for nothing but the best. Graham wished he knew how to unlock her positive, peppy side to take on other areas of life.

Coach Kent switched Bryce out for another player. Bryce took a place on the bench, the look on his face matching the one he'd had in the store on Black Friday. Though Coach taking him out of the game hadn't been about the missed shot, his look had to be.

About a week had passed since Thanksgiving. Since their interactions over the holiday hadn't been spectacular, Graham had been giving him space in practice. But he had seen the error that led to Bryce's missed shot.

Graham sat one space away from him on the bleacher. "Nice job out there. Just don't let those guys intimidate you out of looking at the net. They've got nothing on you. It'll go in if you put your eyes on the prize."

Without looking for Bryce's reaction, Graham walked away. Hopefully, the encouragement would shoot the directive right past Bryce's defenses. If not, Graham wasn't sure what else to try.

* * *

The determination on Bryce's face as he returned to the court had Piper's heart on the edge of its seat. He needed to make a basket, because when such strong determination met disappointment, discouragement and dejection weren't far behind.

"Let's go, team! Come on, boys!" She clapped as similar cheers went up from the other parents, who had slowly joined Piper in doling out encouragement.

Maybe next time, someone else would even sport face paint. Or maybe that had been a little extreme, but she couldn't resist celebrating Bryce and the alpaca farm that sponsored the team. Graham had given her a full-fledged smile and a thumbs up when he'd seen her. She shouldn't have enjoyed his approval as much as she had.

As the ball moved down the court toward the basket Bryce's team defended, her focus strayed to Graham. He held a clipboard and occasionally marked a note about some detail of the game. Like Bryce, he stayed focused and serious.

When Bryce's team snagged possession of the ball and

sped it back toward their basket, Graham tucked the clipboard under his arm and clapped. "Nice! Good work, guys!"

Excitement mounted among the other parents, too, as Bryce's team zeroed in on the basket. The boy closest to the hoop cast a frantic look around. Instead of shooting, he passed it back to Bryce, who was barely inside the three-point line. The long shot was about to become even harder as the other boys hurried over. Determination still written across his features, Bryce lined up his shot. His tongue stuck out the corner of his mouth as he launched the ball.

Piper held her breath. This one shot, halfway through the game, wasn't the dramatic stuff of sports movies. Not for the team, anyway. But for Bryce, it could impact something much more important than the outcome of a game or a season—his decision to stick with basketball or quit.

Please, Lord. He needs some encouragement.

The ball hit the rim. Bounced. Bounced again. And then fell mercifully through the net.

Piper jumped up with a shout and didn't even realize she'd done it until her foot stung. Bryce averted his eyes—smiling and blushing. She retook her seat.

For once, she had to admit, a prayer of hers had been answered favorably.

As the game got organized again, Bryce stepped near the sideline, and Graham put an arm around his shoulders. He bent so he didn't tower over Bryce, and by his hand motions, he said something about the game. As Bryce jogged to take his place among his teammates, he continued to grin. That was a first—Bryce smiling after an encounter with Graham.

She'd tried to manufacture a moment like this by sending them out together on Black Friday. Apparently, she would've been better off simply waiting. What if her other prayers and worries were also on the Lord's radar? What if answers were already in the works?

Her heart soared like the basketball had a moment ago but then fell short. She'd be a fool to think a single basket was a sign God was about to turn her life around.

* * *

Graham ought to help pack up equipment, but he couldn't resist Piper. When she'd arrived at the game, she'd painstakingly made her way up to the third row of bleachers. The doctor had said that, as long as she wore the boot, she could take a step now and then, but Graham couldn't guess why she'd leveraged the exception when she could've sat at the ground level. Whatever had prompted the decision, he didn't want her descending alone.

He climbed up two rows and extended his hand. "He did great, didn't he?"

Piper hooked her fingers together and looked around, as if to see if anyone else might offer to help her down.

Talk about taking a shot and missing. Graham tried to keep the hot feeling that rose in his chest—Disappointment? Frustration?—from registering on his face as he persisted in holding his hand out to her. To rebuff him, she'd have to make a scene because he wouldn't walk away. He'd offer to help pretty much anyone with a broken foot.

Piper lay her fingers, small and warm, in his hand. Her injured foot forced her to rely on him, because her hand pressed on his as she carefully took one step down and then another. As soon as she reached the wood of the gym floor, she pulled back and rubbed her palm against her pant leg. "Nice job with the team."

"Thanks."

She zipped her coat with an awkward smile. "Bryce *did* do great. You're right. I hope you'll keep working with him."

"Why wouldn't I?"

117

Piper shrugged, non-committal. "I don't know. I'm just saying."

Before he could pursue it, Bryce appeared beside them, eyes brighter than all the Christmas lights popping up around town. "You saw?"

Piper high-fived him. "I did see. Great job. You're going to be a star someday!"

Graham resisted ruffling his hand through the boy's hair. "He's already a star."

As Piper jumped in with more encouragement, Graham looked over the other parents, trying to guess who had agreed to drive Bryce to his grandparents' house. After this, Graham and Piper planned to go together to Second Chances, her to relieve Ally and him to make progress on the furniture. No one headed their way.

"Are we giving Bryce a lift to your grandparents' house?"

"No. Grandpa is picking him up. He insisted he would be out running errands anyway."

"Okay." Coach Kent had his two oldest kids with him today, and they'd already completed most of the required cleanup. "I'll grab my coat, and we can all head out together to see if he's here."

Piper and Bryce got a head start. Once he'd checked in with Kent and gathered his things, he found them in the hall, stopped before the high school's trophy cases.

"Where are the pictures with my dad?" Bryce rested his fingers against the metal that framed the case.

Piper rolled the scooter closer. "Here." She tapped a fingernail on the glass.

Bryce laid down a couple of prints and a white puff of breath as he peered inside. "Cool. That's going to be me someday."

Graham hadn't seen Ryan enough to pick out a seventeen-year-old version of the man he'd arrested in the small photo.

"If you keep playing all the way through, maybe you'll land a spot on the varsity team freshman year."

"Is that what my dad did? I want to be like him."

Piper shot Graham a worried look, but Bryce was talking about basketball, not other activities. Surely, if they kept the focus on the team, it would be good for Bryce to look up to his dad, especially if he had changed as much as Piper said.

Together, they worked their way back to the team photo from Ryan's freshman year.

"Doesn't look like he's in this one," Piper said.

"But think of how proud of you he'd be if you made it freshman year."

Bryce nodded vigorously, and Piper shot Graham a smile over the boy's head. She laid a hand on his shoulder. "We shouldn't keep Grandpa waiting."

Chapter Twenty-Four

"You're eating already?" Piper let her purse fall next to the plastic chair where she was scheduled to spend the next three hours selling bake sale treats.

Lucy lifted her hand to cover her mouth as she both grinned and spoke with her mouth full. "You have to try one of these." With her free hand, she extended a small paper plate of red-swirled squares toward Piper.

"What are they?"

"Red velvet cheesecake brownies." Lucy gulped and lowered her hand. "To die for."

They did sound amazing. Piper scanned the bake sale offerings. Brownies, sugar cookies, cupcakes, and chocolate-covered pretzels were only some of the dozens of options. Positioned near the doors of the department store, hopefully their table would attract a lot of shoppers. If not, the time would drag by, and Piper's jeans wouldn't fit anymore.

Lucy set the plate in front of Piper, swiping a second brownie as she retracted her hand. "I paid for them, and we might as well support the sale."

Piper sampled one. Chocolaty and smooth, this beat out

any bar she could remember trying in the past. Whichever of the boys' moms had baked this up had better be willing to share the recipe.

"All right." Lucy settled back in her chair. She waved at a passing shopper, then glanced at Piper. "I want an update."

"On what?" Piper's brownie was disappearing all too quickly. She found a napkin and set the remainder down, determined to savor it.

"Graham. He's been working in your store for weeks, and he's coaching Bryce—successfully, from what I hear. Tell me he's not growing on you."

He was. Oh, how he was. And yet ... "Not all things that grow are good. Mold, for example."

"Piper Wells. If you wanted me to buy that for a minute, you shouldn't have told me about his coaching and the things he's said to you about fear and gratitude."

"Okay, fine. He's handy to have around, except when he's talking me into going on some random date to prove a point." Piper had enlisted Lucy's help to find said date. Preferably some cowboy from some remote ranch whom she'd never have to face again.

Their first customer approached. They helped the woman settle on a plate of the red velvet brownies and a giant bag of caramel corn.

As the customer left, Lucy slid the cash into the money box. "You seem to have a more positive outlook. I think Graham has something to do with that, and not just because Bryce can do a free throw or layover."

"Lay*up*. But I'm not sure he can do one of those."

"You get the point. I like Positive Piper. I want her to hang around. I want her to grow."

"You sound ridiculous."

Lucy smirked. "Positive Piper wouldn't say things like that to me."

Piper laughed and rolled her eyes. "I am trying to be more grateful and hopeful, but bad things still happen. Let's say I'm more cautiously optimistic than positive."

"So you think you and Graham might have a happily ever after?"

"Sure. Just not together. I'm staying single—except to go on the one date he backed me into, which I still need help with because ..." Because she liked Graham and no one else. "It's slim pickings around here."

"Must not be. Seems like there's been a wedding every couple of weeks around here lately." Lucy broke off a piece of brownie. Was it Piper's imagination, or was she comfort-eating?

Perhaps a change of subject was in order. She picked up the rest of her brownie. "Have you heard Alicia Carver is in town?" Piper had dismissed the first couple of whispers about the pop star visiting Redemption Ridge, but then even Graham, whose job kept him up-to-date on the community, had confirmed it. "Apparently, Jordan Taylor is back with her."

"They're together?"

Piper shook her head. "He's her bodyguard."

"Oh. Good. Last I heard, he'd lost his leg and left the Marines, but he must be doing okay for himself if he's protecting celebrities."

She shrugged and nodded. She'd certainly prefer working with a pop star over surviving a war zone, but then something told her Jordan had a very different skill set.

Lucy's quiet chuckle drew her attention.

"What?"

"I was just wondering what the going rate is for a body-guard, because if anyone could use one, it's the woman who wanders out in front of pickup trucks."

Piper turned the last bite of her brownie between her

fingers, thinking of pitching it at her friend. But it was too good to waste, so she popped it into her mouth. Besides, who was she kidding? Her poor body could use a guard.

They helped another customer, and then she slipped the last of the red velvet brownies on their shared plate. A few more packages of these fabulous treats waited on the table. Maybe she'd buy some for herself. To take home and share with Bryce, of course. Because no reasonable adult would scarf down another plate while manning the sale ... Or would they? Reasonableness was overrated.

Lucy coughed pointedly, drawing Piper's attention upward as Graham slowed at their table.

A plastic shopping bag swung from his right hand. "You two selling or just buying?"

Lucy grinned. "A little of both."

Piper gulped down her mouthful of brownie. She probably shouldn't have fit half the thing in her mouth at once. Her face had to be as red as the swirls in the baked treat. "We recommend the red velvet brownies."

Graham's mouth pulled into a smile more delectable than anything on their table. "Red velvet *cheesecake* brownies."

"Oh. Yeah." Her gaze darted around the table, but she didn't spot any labels. How had he known?

Lucy's laughter only made Piper's face redder. She brushed her fingers over her face, in case the joke was crumbs on her cheeks.

Graham gathered a stack of cookies and paid. "Not all for me. I'm headed into work."

Piper fit the goodies into a bag and handed it to him.

"All right, ladies. See you around. Try and sell all of those." He lifted his chin toward Piper's half-eaten brownie. "I don't want leftovers to take back home."

Of course he'd made them. She should've known.

He smiled that smug, teasing smile of his and headed for the doors, his steps light enough to convey his amusement.

Piper swiped at her cheeks, as though her embarrassment could be wiped away as easily as brownie bits. "You could've told me who made the bars."

Lucy let out a full-fledged laugh. "The fact that you loved them proves my point. Maybe you enjoy him more than you care to admit. And he seemed to get quite a kick out of that, too."

"I was enjoying a recipe, not a romance. And as for him, for wanting me to be more optimistic, he sure enjoys making me squirm."

Lucy's eyes glittered as she stood to help a middle-school-aged boy who neared with a couple of crumpled bills in his grasp. Lucy, of course, was right. If life were different, she could see it. Loving Graham, wanting a family with him.

The brownies would be just the figurative icing on the cake.

* * *

As Graham glanced at his clipboard during basketball practice, a smile crept onto his face as an image of Piper from yesterday popped to mind, her cheek bulging with brownie and then blushing at the sight of him.

He caught himself asking the Lord to keep working on her heart. Waiting for her to change her mind about him certainly fed his prayer life.

He scanned the players, who practiced dribbling. Bryce's brown hair stuck to his forehead. He'd been working hard today.

Graham blew the whistle and explained the next drill, one that involved each of the boys dribbling within the three-point line. As they kept their own ball in play, they tried to knock other players' basketballs out of bounds.

Bryce survived until about the halfway point. Then, one of the others whapped his basketball, and he chased it out. Graham shrunk the area of play for the remaining athletes, then took a place next to Bryce. Instead of pouting like he might've done earlier in the season, the boy watched the drill with interest. He'd come a long way.

"You know, Bryce, you never did tell me what interested you in the team."

He shrugged one shoulder, eyes following the strongest player still on the court. "I want to go to state like my dad. He scored seven baskets there."

Graham shifted his clipboard. Piper said Ryan had been benched from the team right before state his senior year. "Who told you about that?"

"My dad." The bright and determined look on Bryce's face discouraged Graham from setting him straight on the spot. Ryan could've played at the state level his junior year.

Graham would check the facts with Piper. In the meantime, he could manage Bryce's expectations. "State is a good goal to have. Just keep in mind not everyone gets to go. It's a lot of work, and it takes a good team, not just one good player."

Bryce continued watching the drill. "I think we'll be good."

"I hope so." But he hoped more that Ryan had told his son the truth because he didn't want Bryce—or his aunt —disappointed.

Not when Graham was starting to hope for the best.

Chapter Twenty-Five

Noise at the back of the store drew Piper from behind the sales counter. This amount of clunking meant Graham, and not a customer, was entering, but what had he brought in that had resulted in this racket? She hadn't sent him out for anything.

She navigated her scooter around Teddy's pen and advanced to the back hall.

"What do you think?" Graham paused, despite his fully loaded arms. He carried a simple, laminate coffee table that might've come from the nineties. Around one of his wrists, he'd looped a plastic shopping bag featuring a smiley face, which meant he'd been to Charlie's hardware store, in addition to wherever he'd found the table.

"I think someone wanted to cheat on furniture for the auction."

"Cheat?" Graham lowered the coffee table a few inches.

How much did the sticker on the top of it say he'd invested in this? Ten dollars?

"I had envisioned donating nicer pieces. Real wood, with special details. This doesn't have any details. It's a top and four legs that'll take about ten minutes to repaint. And I know cheap laminate when I see it."

"It might be made of composite and laminate, but don't mistake that for flimsy. This thing is heavy." Raising the table again bunched his coat over his biceps. "Sturdy. And with some paint—which will take more than ten minutes, by the way—people will never know the difference." He angled his load into the stockroom. "Plus, I have a plan for a finish that'll have everyone bidding on it."

He set the table in the open workspace. She hadn't realized he'd finished everything else they'd acquired so far, but each piece was neatly stacked at the side of the room and padded with blankets. A navy-blue dresser, an off-white china cabinet, and the matching bed, nightstand, desk, and bookcase. Six of ten pieces, and if this were the seventh, he'd have it done in no time. With only two and a half weeks left, it was good he'd made so much progress, but what plan wouldn't result in the coffee table being the black sheep of their offerings at the auction?

Piper scooted close enough to look inside the bag, which Graham had set on top of the table. "Spray paint? They're supposed to be Second Chances 'signature pieces.' My signature isn't spray paint."

"Take a closer look."

The can rattled as she turned it to read the label. "It's brown. That's not a selling point."

"It's copper with a hammered finish. I used it on the vents in my house last year. It's nice."

"For a vent, maybe."

He gave her a withering look. "If you spray on too much, it runs. The hammered finish and the metallic copper combine to look like glossy tree bark. I had to redo one of the vents because I did it on accident, but it'll make a great tabletop."

"That—" She bit her lips together, shutting in her skepticism when he shot her another warning glance.

"If you don't like it, I'll donate this to the auction myself and we can do something different for your tenth piece."

"Okay." Piper put her hands up in surrender. "While you were out thrifting, did you find any other pieces we can use?"

"An old full-length mirror in a wooden frame with a stand. A funky cabinet thing. Half of the top opens for unknown reasons, but shut it and it's a cabinet with sliding doors someone might use as a TV stand or for storage. An old wooden rocking chair that's going to be a bear to sand because of all the dowels. And a four-person dining table."

"That's four. One extra. You knew I'd be skeptical about the coffee table."

"I'm skeptical the hammered paint will dry in time. It has to go on thick to run the way I want. If it's not dry, we'll need another option, and I guess you'll be stuck with a reminder of me." Graham stepped around her, presumably to go back out for the other items.

She maneuvered the scooter to follow. "Are you going to be able to carry this all in alone?"

"Would you help if I said no?"

Before she had to answer, Cody's shape darkened the back door, and Graham swung it open so his friend could carry in the mirror. Working together, the men piled the new pieces in the stockroom, and Cody left again.

Graham lifted the coffee table to better center it on the tarp they used to protect the floor. The motion pulled his T-shirt taut against the muscles of his back and arms. He'd always believed in staying fit for duty, and apparently that hadn't changed in the last two years. Not that she hadn't noticed before this, but—

"What colors and hardware do you want on those?" Straightening, he motioned toward the new collection. "I'll pick up the rest of the supplies on my next trip to Charlie's."

Right. Furniture. Charlie's. Auction. All things she had more business focusing on than Graham's level of fitness. She sized up the new arrivals. He had chosen well. Except the coffee table, each piece fit the aesthetic she'd envisioned.

She found a scrap of paper on the supply table and jotted down a shopping list.

"Who are you taking on your date?"

She dotted a single *i* on her list three times. "My date?"

He leaned against the edge of the table on her good side, trapping her between him and her scooter. Not that he looked like he was trying to corner her. His expression reflected casual curiosity. Was this his idea of small talk?

"With the auction and Thanksgiving, I've been too busy to think about it."

He nodded slowly, studying her as if he could see right through her.

She ought to confess her feelings.

He'd shoot her down, which would dampen her growing affection for him.

Unfortunately, the awkwardness would likely also ruin their friendship.

Less than three weeks remained until the auction and Christmas, and the prospect of running the store in January without him nearby already sounded like drudgery. What would she do when he wasn't hanging around, keeping her company all the time?

He straightened and turned toward the table, a move that brought his arm close enough for his body heat to radiate through the sleeve of her sweater. Or was she imagining that? She glanced up, but he was rifling through the supplies on the table, not focusing on her. She could rarely get away with anything in his presence because he always kept an eye on whoever he shared space with. Except now. She relished the opportunity to study him up close.

His long eyelashes hooked upward in a way a lot of women went to trouble to achieve. He'd once complained about his elementary school librarian complimenting his eyelashes, but Piper understood where the woman had come from. On a little boy, it must've been cute. On a man, the feature added a touch of softness to the serious set of his eyes, the chiseled planes of his cheeks, and the shadow on his jaw that would darken into stubble if he didn't shave tomorrow.

It was definitely warm in here.

"Did Ryan go to state?" With this latest unexpected question, the room temperature dropped back to a reasonable sixty-eight degrees. He opened a new package of sandpaper for the electric sander.

"No." She'd moved a step sideways to allow for more reasonable personal space, but the scooter was too awkward. She fiddled with the pen, too distracted to worry about the list. "Didn't I tell you he was benched?"

"His senior year." He tore open the packet and pulled out one of the disks. "Did he go other years?"

"Ryan's senior year was the first time in something like eight or ten years the team qualified."

"Huh." Graham frowned and stuck the new disk on the head of the sander.

"Why do you ask?"

"Bryce is under the impression his dad made seven baskets at state."

"Where'd he get that idea?"

"Either Ryan lied, or Bryce misunderstood." Graham set down the sander and turned toward her, hip against the table, arms crossed. "Whatever the case, that's why Bryce went out for the team."

"Oh, no. When I tell him the truth ..."

"I know." He touched her elbow. "I was thinking we should wait. If we tell him during the off-season, he'll have a couple of months to think about it before we convince him to play again next year."

"We?" They were a team now? Did he see their relationship going beyond the auction?

He lowered his hand but didn't move back out of her space. "You wanted me to mentor him."

She averted her gaze from his chest and arms, her mind from memories of how those arms felt around her. Unfortunately, she chose to focus on his eyes, which studied her with a careful concern that sent a giddy wave through her core. The pen tipped from her fingers and landed on the table.

Focus, Piper. Focus.

Chiding herself did little good. Focus was the whole problem; hers didn't seem to want to pry itself from Graham. She slow-blinked and scratched her neck, formulating a response. "I should talk to Ryan. Find out where all this is coming from."

He nodded and kept watching her.

Thoughts of Bryce tumbled away from her, and she found herself asking again the question she'd never sent to Lucy—*Graham and I don't work. But why was that again?*

"Don't look so worried." He rested his fingers against her cheekbone and gently touched his thumb to the space between her eyebrows.

She consciously relaxed her furrowed brow. "It's just that …" That they shouldn't be together. Why not? What had they been talking about? Oh. Right. Bryce. "What if this comes between you and Bryce?"

"That would bother you?"

"Well, yes."

"Because you want me to mentor him." Graham moved

closer, their bodies nearly touching, his hand lingering near her jawline.

"Because if you two get along ..."

"Then ...?"

"Then ..." She rested her hands on his chest. She shouldn't linger like this, but the corner of his mouth hooked up, and his breath fanned her cheek.

She stumbled enough to recognize the moment of no return in both physical and emotional circumstances. Such a point hadn't yet happened here. She could still catch herself. She could back away.

Only she didn't. "Then something like this could happen." She'd never more happily surrendered to gravitational pull as when she allowed her body to lean into his. Warmth passed between them as she slid her fingers into the soft, short hair at the nape of his neck.

His lips met hers for a gentle kiss that seemed to ask if this was the something she'd had in mind. Yes, and then some. She conveyed her answer by tightening her hold on him.

They'd done this before. She thought she knew what she was in for. Except, as his mouth claimed hers, she found time had faded her memories of their previous kisses to black and white. This experience blazed in living color. The blue of security, the red of attraction, the yellow of joy, the green of a fresh beginning. The sensations and emotions spun so fast, she'd end up on the floor if not for his arms around her, strong and centering.

When Graham pulled back, he couldn't seem to decide whether to focus on her lips or her eyes, and he didn't drop his hands from around her. "Bryce and I will be okay. *I* will be okay. You can trust this."

She nodded, willing herself to believe him. But already, the logic was wearing thin. She fumbled for the pen she'd dropped.

Graham took another step back, releasing her, his smile fading into a more neutral expression. He returned his focus to the sander. He drew a deep breath that may or may not have hitched once. Perhaps the kiss had affected him as much as her, despite his forever calm and cool demeanor.

"Once you talk to Ryan, we can decide together how to proceed?" The upward hook of his voice, making his statement a question, was a nice gesture. One that had probably not come naturally to take-action Graham.

"Sure." She'd spent the last two years figuring out how to handle a myriad of parenting situations alone. Having help this time was an immense relief.

But a romance? For the space of the kiss, she'd believed him that if he and Bryce could get along, they might one day be a family. But Bryce was only one obstacle keeping them apart.

Her glued-together heart wouldn't withstand another tragedy. And the only way to ensure it wouldn't have to was to keep away from exactly the kind of feelings Graham Lockhart and his mountain-top-blue eyes kept stirring up.

Chapter Twenty-Six

P iper wouldn't believe it if she weren't staring at it, but Graham's coffee table had turned out well. He'd left it propped against a wall, tipped the long way so the texture of the paint would run the length of the piece. The result resembled tree bark as promised, though in a much better way than she'd imagined. After what Teddy had done to the legs of her own coffee table, she wouldn't mind having this one, with its creamy legs and coppery, swirly top, in her living room.

The puppy extended his nose toward the fresh paint, and Piper pulled back on his leash, remembering what Graham had said about how long it would take to dry.

"What do you think?" Graham had gone out for lunch, and she hadn't realized he would return so soon. He carried a paper bag in one hand, a drink carrier with two cups in the other.

She thumbed toward the table. "It's not half bad. And it's already dry."

He set his load on a side table and spread a fresh blanket over the top of the one he'd been using as a tarp. "To a light touch. But I pressed on it this morning. I rubbed out the mark I made the best I can, but if you look closely, I suspect my fingerprint is going to be there forever."

Piper grinned. "A police officer should know better than to leave fingerprints behind."

He snorted as he removed his coat. Once he'd draped the garment over the back of a chair, he brought his lunch to the center of the blanket. "I got some for you too."

She'd brought a can of chicken noodle soup, but whatever deep-fried goodness he'd brought smelled a million times better.

"A picnic in the stockroom, huh?" She let go of the scooter and stepped gingerly on her bad foot.

Before she did it again, Graham took her hand, his grip warm and firm. Her stomach twisted at the contact, and she lifted her eyes. He met her gaze, then blinked and looked away. He managed to avoid further eye contact until after he'd helped her settle opposite the food bag from him.

"Did you get a haircut?" he asked.

"Just styled it differently." She lifted her fingers to her hair, which she'd worn down for once. She wished she hadn't thought of him as she'd smoothed styling cream through the strands to keep frizz at bay, but she had.

And her feelings for him went deeper than decisions about her hair and clothes. Graham's handsome face and steady presence were never far from her mind.

Thankfully, he hadn't made any advances since their kiss. They'd never even talked about it. He passed Piper her sandwich and fries—holding the food high enough that Teddy's ever-probing nose couldn't reach—without so much as brushing her hand.

She took a sip of her drink and unwrapped her sandwich. The distance was good.

But what had prompted it on his end?

When Teddy nosed toward her food again, Graham pinned the leash underfoot so the puppy couldn't steal a bite. Teddy circled and plopped down on the blanket, resigned to the distance.

As Piper should be where Graham was concerned. But something must be bothering him, or he would've made another move. Or at least talked to her about that kiss. Which, she would've admitted if he'd asked, had been as fabulous as it was unrepeatable.

But why did he agree? She didn't know how to ask. "What are your Christmas plans this year?"

"I'm staying for the auction on the twenty-third, so I'll leave Christmas Eve morning to drive back home, stay just long enough for the normal traditions, then make it back for a shift Wednesday night."

If her goal was to quell her feelings for him, she should've asked about something else. Thinking about him going home for Christmas brought back fond memories of the year she'd accompanied him. Her own family Christmases had changed irreparably the year her parents had died, and celebrating with Graham's father, brother, sister, and their families had been as close as she'd come to recreating the wide-eyed wonder and joy of her childhood celebrations.

She'd lain awake the last night of the trip, down the hall from where Graham slept in his childhood bedroom, longing for him to propose so she could become a permanent part of this wonderful family. To share a future like that with the man she loved.

If he'd asked then, before Ryan's arrest and poor Bryce's tough adjustment period brought reality slamming back, she would've said yes.

"What's that look?"

She shook her head and cleared her expression. "No look. Um. Well, my plans are also the usual with one major bonus. I have an appointment on the twenty-second where the doctor says I'll probably be cleared to stop using the boot."

"Wow. Congrats. Big day. Things will begin to go back to normal."

Normal? Disappointment swooped through her.

Normal meant no Graham.

Would it be so wrong to stretch out their time together? "I have to go around and pick up the money from candy bar sales next Saturday. Want to come?" She gulped, realizing he wouldn't agree to extra time together without a practical reason. "Carrying back whatever doesn't sell would be awkward with the scooter. I was going to go at ten."

Graham shrugged and nodded. "Sure."

"What are you going to do with all your time after Christmas, when things go back to normal?"

"Haven't thought much about it. Have you? Thought about who you're taking on that date?"

Her skin heated through faster than a tomato tossed into a wildfire. "I suppose I should make a plan, but it's going to be awkward. I'm not interested in anyone."

"A deal's a deal."

"We hardly made a deal. It was more of ... a way to prove I trust God, I guess? But that doesn't accomplish the purpose, because how much trust does it take to go out for dinner with a man I'm not interested in?"

"You'd have to go with someone you *are* interested in." His gaze met hers for a heated second.

At least, it felt heated on her end.

After a few bites of his Philly cheesesteak, he wiped his mouth. "Speaking of. About the other day. I'm sorry. I know you don't see us like that."

Her head jerked in a nod, as if her body were fighting to convince her mind that he was right. "Do you?"

He studied her, his face giving nothing away.

"I hope we can still be friends." Her statement was a test.

Graham returned to his food. "As your friend, your dating life is none of my business."

He was stepping back, not pursuing her.

She might've been asking for that, yet something inside her dropped and broke like a glass Christmas ornament.

Chapter Twenty-Seven

Graham entered Second Chances through the front door on Saturday morning. The choice was strategic. First, since they were picking up candy bars and money, he wouldn't be parked on Main Street longer than the two-hour time limit imposed on this block. Second, Piper would expect him to enter from the other way, giving him the opportunity to surprise her.

"Good morning." Piper's greeting came from the direction of the sales counter. She must've offered the salutation blindly, because a rack of long dresses blocked the view. For security reasons, she ought to relocate the display, but the cover served his purposes. By the time he rounded the display, he was only three feet from the register. Plenty close to watch the rose-pink bloom on her cheeks.

She claimed to want the friend zone, but he doubted she blushed at the sight of her other friends.

"Ready to collect some candy bars?" She stood and rubbed her hands in overdone excitement.

He helped her into her coat instead of calling her on it. He liked flustering her. Especially when she got flustered enough to forget her fears and kiss him like she had in the stockroom.

And what a kiss. He'd been craving a repeat ever since.

Thing was, he didn't trust decisions made by a flustered mind. Though her fear was as strong as a chain, it behaved more like an elastic band, stretching sometimes, but forever pulling her back. Meanwhile, he had no desire to set himself up for rejection again. Pursuing her heart before she dealt with her fear would result in another disaster. He had to be careful this time. Patient. Their next kiss wouldn't be until after the cord had broken for good.

Even if the wait killed him.

Which it wouldn't. Not directly, anyway, but—

"Ready?"

He was blocking Piper's path from behind the sales counter. "Yes. Do we need the cart for this?"

"I called the stores. Almost all of them sold out of the candy bars, so, as long as you can carry one box, no cart necessary. Think you can handle it?" She squeezed his biceps as she rolled by with her scooter.

He lifted an eyebrow.

Her blush deepened.

He hid his smile by moving ahead to hold the door for her. For shorter distances, she'd been forgoing the scooter, but today's route would take them several blocks. He let her set the pace as they started down Main Street.

Overhead, clouds moved in, the first signs of a storm predicted to blanket Redemption Ridge in ice and snow overnight. Hopefully, the precipitation would hold off until after their errand.

The sweater displayed in the front window of JoJo's Scrapbooking and Yarn had a button pinned to it, advertising the benefit auction for the Rasinskis. A small paper sign tented in front of it said, "Bid on this sweater!"

Graham wondered if it'd occurred to any small business owner besides Piper to donate not one or two but ten items. He pulled open the door for her to precede him into the shop.

Back at Second Chances, the last of the furniture waited for him to finish. With her foot becoming less painful, Piper had sanded down the pieces he hadn't gotten to yet and had also completed some of the priming. An impressive accomplishment, given she still wasn't back to one hundred percent. If not for the accident, she would've been fine all on her own, even if the commitment would've daunted anyone else in town.

"What inspired you to donate ten items, anyway?" he asked.

"For the auction?" She shrugged. "It's a young family, and they need help. Riley's the cutest."

"There's that soft spot you have for kids."

She glanced at him. "I think it's been growing lately."

JoJo appeared in his peripheral vision and stole her attention away.

Graham didn't take his eyes off Piper. She could've argued with him. In the past, to signal loud and clear that she didn't want kids, she would've. If she was hinting like this, she might be closer to overcoming her fears than he'd realized. They might come out on the other side of all this as a couple. One day, Lord willing, they could have a family. Everything he'd wanted and thought he'd never get.

"Hi, guys." JoJo's bright greeting jerked him out of the future and back to the present.

Which wasn't such a bad place to be, considering he was with Piper and her growing soft spot for kids.

JoJo wore a canvas apron with knitting needles stashed in one of the pockets. The even knit of her sweater could pass for store-bought, but undoubtedly, she'd crafted it herself. "Here for candy bar money?"

"Yup." Piper's tone matched JoJo's cheer. She browsed the impulse purchases near the register. "Are you ready for Christmas?"

"Mostly." JoJo opened the till and took an envelope from under the money tray. "How about you? Don't tell me you'll still be in a boot."

"Nope. Comes off Friday. I can't wait." Piper accepted the envelope and slid it into the manila mailer she'd brought. "Having it off will be the best Christmas gift I get this year."

JoJo glanced at Graham as if to ask whether he planned any extravagant gifts that might compete. When he didn't issue a challenge, she returned her focus to Piper. "Don't be surprised if building back up the muscle you lost takes a while. It might be painful. Be gentle with yourself."

"The doctor gave me rehab exercises, some of which I can do already." Piper nudged her finger through the assortment of buttons in the dish by the checkout. "But yeah, she warned me. And I get to wear tennies with the thickest, stiffest soles you've ever seen." With a self-deprecating laugh, she tucked her hair behind her ear.

He hadn't put much thought into her having trouble after the boot came off. Maybe she'd need help with a few things, giving him an excuse to keep dropping by the store.

"Good girl. Follow those orders." JoJo turned to Graham. "So we know what's on Piper's Christmas wish list. What about yours?"

Piper's heart. That was the extent of his list. He forced a relaxed smile. "I'm looking forward to the auction. The Rasin-skis' expressions when they see the community's generosity will probably be the best gift I get this year."

Piper gave him a proud smile, and he let her handle the rest of the small talk with the shop owner.

Whether or not she needed his help around her store, they

could remain friends. As a friend, could he invite her over for dinner? Or was that too much like a date?

After a few more pleasantries, Graham again got the door for Piper.

Almost as soon as she'd straightened her front tire to point herself down the walk, she said, "Hey, so, um ..."

His breath froze. She'd save him a lot of trouble if she'd go ahead and ask him on the date she'd agreed to.

"I spoke to Ryan," she said.

Oh. Not what he'd hoped to hear, but important, nonetheless. "And?"

"He did tell Bryce he played in the state game. The conversation happened shortly after his arrest, and I guess he was embarrassed of his situation, so he embellished. A lot. He apologized and said he'll tell Bryce the truth the next time he sees him."

"When will that be?"

"A week from today. I'm taking him between setting up furniture in the morning and the auction that evening."

"Maybe the busy schedule will keep Bryce from stewing on it."

Piper chewed her lip. "Do you think he'll quit the team?"

"I imagine that'll depend on Ryan's delivery." He didn't hold out much hope a man with Ryan's history could soften such news. But then, he hadn't been interacting with Ryan and didn't know how he'd changed.

"It might go okay." She bumped her shoulder into his, as if to tell him to cheer up. "If not, you and I can talk to him."

A sense of peace lifted his lips. She was hoping for the best and making plans with him. If those cords of fear hadn't broken yet, they would soon, and he needed to save himself a front-row seat. "What if you and Bryce came over for dinner next Friday?" he asked. "Bring Teddy too. It's the day before the auction, and we should celebrate finishing our work and you getting your boot off. Besides, that'll let me get in some quality time with Bryce, so we have more to go on if things don't go well with Ryan the next day."

Piper cocked her head and smiled absently toward the street before them. "Sure."

It wasn't a date. Yet the victory kept him smiling through the rest of their stops, buoying his mood as his morning with Piper wound down. They returned to Second Chances, and though he'd rather find reasons to hang around, he had a shift in a few hours and some tasks to tackle at home beforehand.

Thanks to the storm, the roads turned icy as night fell and the rain turned to snow, but Redemption Ridge tended to get quiet pretty quick after dark. He parked to work on paperwork near the outskirts of town, where the higher rural limit dropped to city speeds. Prominent under a streetlight, the cruiser would serve as an extra reminder to drivers to slow down. Not much longer and he could head back to the precinct and—

"Patrol Three, Five, and Six." The dispatcher's voice came over the radio, brisk as she called for three officers, including Graham. "Robbery in progress at Quick Stop, six-two-four Chambers."

The gas station was just down the street. Graham hit the button on his speaker microphone. "Patrol Three. En route from Chambers and First."

Even before Officers Casper and Hughes confirmed their locations, Graham knew he'd be first on the scene.

As he pulled onto the road, dispatch provided more information. "Be advised, witness states subject is a white male in a dark hoodie, armed with a handgun."

Chapter Twenty-Eight

"Hughes and I roll up around the same time, and there's cash everywhere." Officer Casper spread her hands, hamming up the retelling of the call they'd just wrapped up. The new shift of officers, Cody among them, hung on her every word. "The wind kicks up and bills blow around like in one of those money-grab games. In the center of this cyclone of money, Lockhart is already cuffing the guy."

As the others clapped his shoulder in celebration, Graham laughed. "It was kind of anti-climactic. He slipped on the ice as he ran from the store."

If not for that, Graham would've waited for the other officers before taking action, but the Lord had been kind. On the drive over, the dispatcher had relayed that the witness had seen the subject enter the store alone and that the vehicle he'd driven appeared empty. So when the lone perpetrator had slipped on the ice and fallen face-down on the pavement, Graham had moved in before the robber could recover the gun that had skidded away.

But of course, Casper wasn't done with her story yet.

"The first thing the guy does when Graham stands him up is try to catch a passing twenty with his teeth."

"He get it?" someone asked.

Casper scoffed. "No, but halfway to the car, he decides maybe being arrested isn't his favorite idea in the world and starts putting up a fight in that skating rink of a parking lot."

"I always thought Lockhart would make a good figure skater," Cody quipped.

Casper grinned. "Less graceful, but more fun to watch."

At least someone enjoyed it. The tussle had laid Graham out on his back and whacked his head against the pavement. He had a lump and some bruises to show for it, but thankfully no signs of a concussion. Hughes and Casper had moved in to help, and the rest of the call had gone without incident.

When the story wrapped up and the group moved off, Cody hung back. "Casper's impressed."

Was that a flare of jealousy in his friend's voice? Graham glanced up from the computer. Cody had his arms crossed over his uniform, gaze on Graham.

He shrugged. "I was in the right place at the right time."

"So what's the problem?"

"No problem."

Cody's eyes narrowed. After a few beats, he asked, "What'd Piper say about it?"

"It's the middle of the night. I haven't told her yet."

And he didn't want to. She might be taking a more hopeful view of life, but the optimism might not hold up against a handgun. He hadn't been in real danger this time, but she specialized in what-ifs.

"So tomorrow?" Cody prompted. "You'll see her at church."

Graham cleared his throat, but he couldn't agree to ruin everything. Not when he was just getting her back.

Cody looked at the ceiling, sighed, then returned an unimpressed gaze to Graham. "She's going to hear. If not through the grapevine Casper's growing, then from the paper. An event like this will warrant a press release."

Graham rested his arm on his desk, but the position hit the angry bruise on his elbow earned during the arrest. He shifted. "The press release won't name the officer. Besides, nobody reads the paper anymore."

"Plenty of people read the paper, and everyone at the station knows what happened. Like it or not, you're a hero."

To everyone but the one person who mattered. "When I tell her something like that happened and I was involved—and especially that the guy got the better of me by knocking me down—I'll confirm her fears."

"You don't have a choice."

Graham scrubbed his fingers through his hair. "I know."

"Besides, what are you supposed to do? Quit your job? Hide what it entails forever? Even if you could, you can't avoid or hide every injury, illness, or threat for the rest of your life."

"She's already more optimistic. I just was hoping we'd have smooth sailing long enough that she'd really trust God again."

"Smooth sailing doesn't result in deeper trust. We learn we can rely on God when we choose faith in stormy seas." Cody had a point, even if he added flair to the last two words, as if he thought he deserved an award for carrying the metaphor through. "If you're not the one to break the news, it'll be a lot worse."

More truth, plain and simple. "I'll talk to her."

"Sooner than later."

Graham nodded. As soon as he could find the right way to say it.

* * *

Graham rehearsed what he'd say to Piper as he drove to her house on Monday morning. The sun slanted yellow between the houses and illuminated the snow with a warm glow.

Too bad his mood was as dark as a storm cloud at the prospect of telling Piper about the robbery. Finishing up the furniture would give him an excuse to continue to spend time in her store, and maybe she'd fall for him despite herself.

But only if God helped her past her fear.

He sighed as he shifted his truck into park. After a knock, he let himself in the back door. The scooter waited at the top of the stairs. He deposited it in the truck and came back. Teddy skittered across the kitchen floor, all paws and clumsy balance.

Piper would have a seventy-pound dog on her hands in no time. He clipped a leash on the puppy, then set the ball of energy back on the floor, unable to match that level of enthusiasm and spirit when he was about to lose Piper. Again. "All set?"

"Yes." She stepped in from the living room without a scooter or a crutch. Slow and stiff, she worked her way toward him.

Since what he had to tell her could result in this being the last time they did this, Graham took her hand as she braved the first stair. He held her hand down the steps and all the way to the truck.

Once they'd settled in the cab, he backed the truck onto the road. "How was your weekend? We hardly got to talk at church yesterday."

"Whose fault is that?" she teased.

"Sorry." He'd arrived late, and then she'd gotten tied up in conversations afterward. He could've waited for her to wrap them up, but he'd thought the story of the robbery would be best told in the privacy of Second Chances this morning. Bryce was at school, not waiting for her to feed him lunch, and since the store didn't open for a couple of hours, they could talk as long as they needed to.

"Well, if you must know, Bryce and I had a bit of a rough patch. He told me he'd rather live with his dad. That he hates it with me."

"He's a kid. Don't take it personally."

"It's hard not to. And the whole thing has me wondering what'll happen when Ryan tells him the truth. I mean, if the road's this bumpy now, what'll he do when he's mad at his dad, too? Kent mentioned my brother was mad at the world back in high school. What if Bryce ends up the same way?"

"Hey." Graham flipped on his signal to turn onto Main Street. "You're not supposed to worry like this, remember?"

He stopped at the sign on the corner and spared her a glance, willing her to recover. He needed her to be able to handle a tiff with Bryce. If she couldn't, what were the odds she'd take the robbery in stride?

"You're right." Her smile seemed rueful. "It's still hard sometimes. I want everything to turn out amazingly for him. I hate feeling like I'm not doing right by him or like no matter what I do, I can't guarantee the future I want for him."

"You're doing a good job, Piper." He put the vehicle back in motion. "Everyone has a rough morning now and then. Don't read too much into each little hiccup."

"Maybe. He does seem a lot better today." A block passed. "Anyway, how about your weekend?"

The innocent question tied his organs in knots. This had to be how people felt when he pulled them over for a minor traffic violation while they had a carload of contraband. He focused on safely parking behind Second Chances. He had planned to tell her this morning, but how had he planned to word it again? As if spinning the situation would help him any more than it'd help a suspect. He'd been trained to read people, and though Piper might not be able to apply that skill to strangers, she knew how to read him.

Piper's feather-light touch on his forearm should've barely registered through his winter jacket, but his chest jolted like she'd zapped him with a defibrillator. "You seem tense. Is it because the Quick Stop was robbed?"

Another jolt. "You heard?"

She nodded, eyes sad but forehead unfurrowed. "Lucy texted me a picture of the article that ran this morning. I see why you were worried to mention it to me."

"You do?"

Then why was she calm? Perhaps she hadn't been growing attached to him the way he'd imagined she was. The only alternative explanation, almost too good to be true, was she'd learned to trust.

"You thought I'd be upset." For once, Teddy stayed curled up in a sleepy ball, and Piper rubbed behind one of his ears. "I *don't* feel great about it, but at least no one was hurt."

Graham had been hurt, but the tenderness in his elbow and scalp where he'd hit the pavement was already fading. The bruise on his elbow had turned into a kaleidoscope of green and blue. She probably meant she was grateful no one had been shot. "I'm grateful for that too."

The upward tilt of the corners of her mouth gave him courage. He reached across the seat. Resting his wrist on Teddy, he touched her fingers, and she slid her hand into his.

Unbelievable.

"You'll still come for dinner Friday?" He swallowed, remembering the meal wasn't supposed to be a date. "We're still friends?"

She cocked her head, eyeing their hands.

Yeah, maybe he didn't hold hands with his friends, but he couldn't seem to let her go.

She squeezed his hand. "I think it's important for both of us to be honest."

"What do you want to know?"

Eyes lowered, she traced his fingers with her free hand. "I want to know if, maybe, on Friday ..." She was killing him. He ended the statement a hundred ways before she finally got around to it. "If it would be okay with you if it were just you and me." On the last word, she lifted her gaze.

He couldn't imagine a clearer indication that she'd conquered her fears than her reaction to the robbery. "More than okay."

Her smile turned impish. "I did promise, after all, to go on a date."

"I don't know. It needed to be with someone you cared about for it to matter."

She squeezed his hand. "Then it has to be you."

"I'm in." He was *all* in.

If it weren't for the way she released him and opened her door, he would've kissed her. But then, she was out of the cab, and he wasn't about to let her get her scooter from the bed of the truck alone.

As he rounded the vehicle, he dismissed the niggling worry that the conversation about the robbery had been too easy.

With all the hard things in life, too easy sounded just about right.

Chapter Twenty-Nine

P iper's stop at Charlie's Hardware on Friday would be quick. In and out.

And nothing terrible would happen, unlike the last time she'd tried to make only a quick stop at Charlie's. God was good, and He was taking good care of her. She could trust Him. Life was looking up.

Way up.

She flexed her ankle. Half an hour ago, the doctor had cleared her to stop using the boot. This trip to the store marked the first she'd driven herself anywhere in weeks.

God was good—and in more ways than she would've dared to ask.

An outfit for tonight's dinner with Graham was laid out at home, waiting for her to finish this errand. She would layer a camel-colored cardigan over a simple green dress, paired with her trusty cowboy boots. Worn in to perfection, the footwear choice should be easy enough on her feet for a couple of hours, especially since the night wouldn't involve much walking.

She pushed open her car door and plopped her new, white

tennis shoe—with an extra thick sole per the doctor's instructions—right into a pile of parking lot slush.

When her familiar pessimism rose up, she dismissed it mid-sentence. A pile of slush wasn't awful. The minor inconvenience would do her a favor, even. She liked clean shoes, but not the shining white of a brand-new pair like this one.

She shook the icy sludge from her foot and continued inside.

Charlie met her at the paint counter. The older man, with his droopy cheeks and eyes, reminded her of a friendly hound. "No boot!"

She grinned. "I feel like a new woman."

"Look like one, too. You're all ..." He fluttered his wide fingers, his vocabulary apparently failing him. "Shiny," he finally supplied.

That was probably the lip gloss, which she'd applied today to test how it looked before dinner with Graham.

"I need a pint of *Mint Candy* and one of *Lolly Poppy*." Hard to believe these customer-favorite paint colors wouldn't go on auction pieces—those were all ready to go with the final topcoat curing. Cody and Graham would haul everything to the high school tomorrow.

She'd meet them to oversee the arrangement of the pieces, and then all that would be left to do was attend the event and try not to hover over the silent bidding sheets to see how much the pieces brought in for the Rasinskis.

"You and Graham are quite the pair."

"Excuse me?"

Charlie gave an easy smile, as though she was cute to pretend cluelessness. Apparently, the residents of Redemption Ridge knew she and Graham were well on their way back to being an item.

"Well, what with you and the truck incident, then his wrestling match with that crook." Charlie spoke like this was common knowledge, and like he was simply jogging her memory. "You both get yourselves into the worst binds. What a good thing he was wearing a vest, huh?"

The balloon of her good mood popped. Had the incident at the gas station been the start of a string of robberies? Had something new happened, with Graham at the center of it this time? "What crook?"

"The guy." Charlie lifted his hands as if he couldn't imagine she didn't know. "The one who tried to rob the Quick Stop. Coupla days ago?"

"Oh." So not a new event. Lucy had texted her the article about the Quick Stop robbery. If Piper had better balance, she'd kick herself for not looking it up and reading it. She'd dismissed the event as harmless when Lucy said they arrested the man without incident as he left the gas station.

But if it'd gone without incident, why did anyone need to wear a bulletproof vest? And why had no one mentioned Graham's direct involvement or a gun? Suddenly, Graham's shock over her even-keel reaction made a lot more sense. She should've asked him more questions.

Her foot ached. The news of a threat had tensed her whole body, all the way down to her toes. She exhaled slow and even, willing the panic to subside. She'd seen Graham since the robbery. He was alive and well. And whatever happened, God was in control.

Charlie studied her, looking about ready to wave a hand in front of her face and ask if she was okay.

She forced a wobbly smile. "I'm glad it ended well."

"Lucky thing the guy slipped on the ice, coming out of the store. I can't imagine charging him and wrestling for the gun would've worked any other way. As it was, taking one to the vest must've smarted something awful. Did it leave a bruise?"

During the year they'd dated, Piper had once dropped by Graham's house unannounced and found him working on a landscaping project shirtless. She probably wasn't supposed to dwell on the memory, but the strong contours of his torso were burned in her mind. At Charlie's question, a gruesome bruise spread black tendrils across his chest, deathly purple and red blooming over his heart.

"You okay?" Charlie asked. "Sorry. It's probably hard to talk about him getting shot. That'd traumatize anyone. I wasn't trying to ..." The older man squinted, chewed his lip, and then his expression brightened. "Anyway, he's a hero! I wouldn't wanna do what he does, run toward the guy with the gun instead of away, right? Glad the good Lord made men like him."

The world swayed. The sound of panting registered—from her own mouth. She pressed a hand to her chest, pleading for God to have mercy, for her life to return to the sense of safety and hope she'd had only moments before. But the ghastly image of Graham wouldn't budge from her mind, far more real than the sense of safety she'd walked in with. She wandered from the paint counter.

Charlie called after her, but she couldn't decipher his words through the ringing in her ears. She fled to her car and collapsed into tears.

Chapter Thirty

Graham cracked open the oven. A dish of cheesy potatoes bubbled on the top rack, spots browning in the center. Below, the dinner rolls baked, also moments from golden perfection. He checked the time.

Piper ought to arrive in three minutes. If someone had told him two months ago he'd be getting back together with her in time for Christmas, he would've put them through a field sobriety check. Yet here he was.

He touched the foil covering the resting steak. Still warm. He took the green beans from the microwave and dumped them from the steamer bag into a bowl.

The doorbell rang, and Banjo rose with a *woof*.

Two minutes early. Graham wiped his sweaty palms on his shirt as he edged around the dog to get to the front entry. "Mind your manners, or I'll build a doghouse just to put you in it."

Undeterred, Banjo swayed closer, attention on the door.

Graham took what was supposed to be a calming breath and swung it open.

Piper stood on the step. Beneath her coat, she wore a green

dress and cowboy boots, the kind that appeared more suited for fashion than a hard day's work. A definite upgrade from the black monstrosity. He lifted his gaze to offer her a smile, but then found the one mismatched part of her appearance: her swollen, red eyes.

Concern whooshed through him like a wildfire. He drew her into a hug. Whatever the wrong, he'd right it. No matter how far he had to go or who he had to put in their place, he would come through for her. "What's wrong?"

She nestled her head against his chest, her arms banded around his waist like she didn't plan to let go anytime soon. Suited him.

Cradling her to himself with one arm, he drew her inside and shut out the cold. Vying for attention, Banjo nudged Piper's thigh. Graham snapped his fingers twice, got the dog's attention, and pointed for him to go lie down. With a longing look at Piper, the dog obeyed the silent command. That done, Graham bent his head and brushed her hair back from her face where it remained against his chest. "Tell me."

She squeezed her eyes tighter. "Someone said you got shot."

"That's awful. Who?"

She shook her head, her cheek bumping against him. "I knew it wasn't ... I mean, I thought ..." She sniffed and shifted until she could smooth both palms over his chest. The warmth of her touch registered through the fabric of his shirt over his heart. "I knew it wasn't true, because he said it happened during the Quick Stop robbery, and I had seen you since then. Besides, he said it hit your vest, so even if you had been shot, it would've been okay, right? But he asked if you have a bruise."

The way she glided her hands over his heart made more sense. "The only bruise I have from Quick Stop is the one on my elbow, from where I fell on the ice."

"Because you were wrestling with an armed man?" She bit her trembling lip.

He cupped her cheeks. When her brown eyes blinked up at him, he fought the urge to kiss her and draw her in. Instead, he wiped away one of her tears with his thumb and started from the beginning. "I was called to a robbery in progress. I was close, so I arrived first. The 911 caller said the subject had a gun, so we—me and the others who were called —would normally gather information before determining how to proceed. As I pulled up, the subject ran from the building, a grocery bag in one hand and his handgun in the other. That night was icy, and he slipped two steps out the door. Fell, dropped the bag of money and the pistol. I had a small window to grab him before he would've recovered the gun and run off into the surrounding residential areas. He was cooperative as I approached, put his hands behind his head, didn't try to get up. As I was putting the cuffs on, the other officers arrived. Partway to the car, he did try to pull away, and we both fell. That's how I bruised my arm. I also hit my head, but neither injury required treatment. I was not shot. By the time I approached him, the man wasn't even armed."

Her chin bunched. "You never said it was you."

"What was me?"

"When we talked about the robbery, you didn't say you were there or that you arrested the robber. You also didn't say he was armed."

Falling on the ice had been less disorienting. "I thought you knew." The word robbery more or less implied a weapon. And he'd had no idea she didn't understand he'd been involved. As he'd told Cody, the press release hadn't included his name, but word of his role in the arrest had spread far and wide. How hadn't she known? Yet ignorance explained her calm reaction.

Here he'd thought the relaxed response had demonstrated how far she'd come.

He'd thought it was proof the Lord had cut the cords of fear.

The tendons of her neck were rigid, and her pulse fluttered against his palm.

He tucked her hair behind her ear and rubbed her shoulders. "I'm okay."

Piper touched his arm. At first, he thought she wanted another hug, but instead, she guided him to rotate it. Cooking had warmed the house, so he'd opted for a short-sleeved polo for the evening. Until she sucked in a breath, he hadn't thought about the choice leaving his still-angry bruise exposed.

"I am okay."

A fresh flood washed into her eyes. "What if he'd overpowered you?"

"When I fell? Casper and Hughes were on site by then."

"He could've gotten your gun, and then—"

"Highly unlikely. He was already cuffed."

"Falling could've really hurt him too. You could've been sued."

He could answer the fear with reason, as he had with the other concerns, but she might have a long list. Each individual worry wasn't the true problem here. Haunting fear was dragging her back again. "You're spiraling into worst-case scenarios over something that's already over. Everyone is safe and well."

She exhaled, shoulders drooping. "Everyone except me."

"Piper." He wanted to crush her into another hug, but she stiffened when he tried to draw her in. She did allow him to take her hand, so he squeezed her fingers. "Let this be another example of God's protection and faithfulness. The situation could've been dangerous, but He worked it out peacefully."

She blinked and tears raced down her cheeks. "I know I'm supposed to have faith. I keep trying. But I can't stand the thought of something happening to you. What if you had been shot?"

He'd thought she'd broken his heart when she'd rejected his proposal, but this was tearing him in two. First, because of her suffering. Second, because he knew where this line of reasoning had led her two years ago. How had he set himself up for another rejection? He'd tried to be careful. "Why are you back to worrying about the bad things instead of being grateful for the good ones?"

"I thought God was turning my life around and the worst was behind me. Behind *us*. But you burned the candle at both ends, helping me while maintaining your own full-time job—an important but dangerous full-time job. You weren't operating at one hundred percent because of me. How can I let you risk continuing that?"

"The parking lot was slick. My fall had nothing to do with how I was *operating*. But for the record, I'd never let something come between me and doing my job well. Too much rides on me being at one hundred percent."

She disentangled her hands from his and hugged her coat around herself.

The move felt like a rejection, and his own heart rate kicked up in response. He'd been in situations like this before, situations where he'd thought he'd done everything right, and yet he ended up alone anyway. "Please, Piper. Trust that God has the best in store for you, despite any pain—past, present, or future."

"I wish it was as easy as choosing that. I keep trying ..." Her gaze seemed hazy as it aimed somewhere below his face. At his chest, maybe? She winced and her hand disappeared behind her back, coinciding with the rattle of the doorknob turning. "I need some time. Just to ..." She exhaled through pursed lips. "Can I take a raincheck on our dinner?"

The question reminded him of the dinner he'd made, the

dishes still in the oven. A dark and toasty scent in the air meant he'd left the potatoes and rolls in too long when he'd abandoned them for this conversation. "That depends."

"On?"

"I thought things were changing and you were looking forward to a future together, open to the idea of marriage and kids someday. But ... are you?"

"You're asking me this now?"

The refusal to answer cut as deeply as any response could've. But she was scared. Traumatized once again by her fears. If they had any chance of their relationship progressing past where it'd fallen apart last time, they needed a new approach. One he prayed the Lord would provide.

He didn't have a whole picture yet of how that might look, but he sensed she needed to know where he stood so she could make informed decisions herself.

"I don't need you to answer tonight, but I do need you to understand I'm not on the fence. I'm not interested in just being friends or casual dating. We've done that. We know where it leads, and I'm all in. I want a future with you. I want a family. I want to support each other through the ups and downs. I want to protect you in every way possible. But you have to choose those things too. If I thought for a minute that switching careers would keep you from feeling the kind of fear you experienced today, I'd do it, but only God can give you the kind of security you need."

Tears lined her eyes. She sniffled and nodded. "That's true. I don't know why it doesn't feel so simple. Why I can't forget all these fears."

"For one, I heard you say you thought God was turning your life around. Trusting Him to bring only the events you want into your life won't work, because He does tell us we'll have trouble."

She shrugged and nodded miserably. "I know. I've asked

Him to take my fears and help me trust, but I can't push them away."

Finally, a new idea occurred to him. One he prayed would bring healing and not more brokenness. "Through Him, you're more than a conqueror. You don't have to forget fear or push it away. Defeat it. Face those what-if questions—ask them all again, but this time, answer them too."

Her eyes went wide, and she tensed. "You want me to dwell on worst-case scenarios?"

"Don't dwell on the heartache. Dwell on the aftermath. Figure out where God will be in the situation, not only in the intangible ways, but also in the practical, real-world tools and support systems He's provided for when worse comes to worst. Not that you should trust your plans over Him—He's sovereign and sometimes He provides in ways we never could've anticipated. But, a lot of the time, He does work through established methods. So take the nebulous unknowns and figure out how you'd cope. Because He's brought you through so much already, and you've coped, and you would do it again. Don't lose sight of the fact that even after a trial, God can make life beautiful again."

"But if you'd died ..."

"Heaven is the most beautiful possibility of all. And for the people who are left behind, God can be in resources like estate planning and community and counseling. Often, through those things and through His word, He provides for us and heals the hurt. And even before we see that happen, He's Emmanuel—with us through every moment of it."

She rolled her lips together, eyes moving as though to track ideas floating between them.

"But me supplying those answers for you won't give you the reassurance you need. Work through these questions. Be realistic about it. Pray about it. See if having answers leads you back here to me."

She focused, her eyes a warm, multi-faceted brown he hoped he'd get to study the rest of his life. "This is an ultimatum?" The question seemed careful, not angry.

They'd really only gotten reacquainted in the last few weeks, and perhaps he was premature in forcing a decision on a committed relationship. But he'd been surprised by rejection a few too many times in his life. "I guess it is. We can regroup after Christmas."

Her eyebrows tented. "That long?"

"Tomorrow's going to be busy with the auction and your visit to see Ryan. I leave for Christmas with my family by eight the next morning."

"Oh." She wrung her hands. "So tomorrow ...?"

"I'll deliver the furniture to the high school in the morning." He didn't mention the auction itself, because he wasn't sure he'd be able to stand being near her if she wasn't his.

She gripped the railing as she made her way down the stairs. He watched until she'd safely pulled away from the curb, then returned to the kitchen and rescued the cheesy potatoes and rolls from the oven. He'd have to peel off the too-dark bits, but otherwise, everything remained edible. If only he had the heart to enjoy the meal alone when he'd meant to share it with the woman he loved.

Love.

He scrubbed his fingers through his hair. If perfect love cast out fear, his was far from perfect, or he wouldn't keep ending up alone.

* * *

Piper startled when her phone's ring broadcast through her car's speakers. She tapped a button on the display to answer Lucy's call.

"Honey, are you okay?" Warm with concern, her friend's

voice filled the car. "Graham texted. He said you might need me?"

"Did he say why?" Her voice shook, and she focused on the road as though her life depended on it. Which, of course, it did. She probably shouldn't be driving in this emotional state. She was a few blocks from Graham's house, but thankfully, in small Redemption Ridge, that meant she was also only a few minutes from home.

"No. What happened? If he broke your heart, he's losing all the points I credited him for texting me."

"I might've broken his." She replayed his declarations of love—he hadn't said the word, but surely that was what his promises and hopes amounted to. Her stomach went woozy with a concoction of attraction and ... and fear. She exhaled through pursed lips. "He says I should face all my what-ifs. Actually answer all those questions I worry about."

As Lucy hesitated, Christmas lights passed outside Piper's windows. One house had set up a nativity scene only a few feet back from the road. Emannuel, Graham had reminded her. God with us through it all.

"I'm not sure that's a rabbit hole you should go down," Lucy said finally.

"I'm already down it. I've been down it for years. I think he might have a point." She certainly didn't feel like a conqueror, let alone *more* than a conqueror, but this fresh idea might lead her to the healing Graham spoke about. Healing she'd read about in the Bible and heard about in testimonies but had never been able to grasp for herself.

Emmanuel. God with us, through it all.

"The day I got hit by the pickup, I wondered how God's protection fit with my experience. I could apply what Graham suggested to the question, 'What if I get hit by a pickup truck?'"

"Piper ..."

"Hear me out. I'm supposed to focus on the answer, not the question. I know this answer because I experienced it. First, a kind acquaintance will give me a ride to the clinic. God was in that. Insurance covers the cost because God blessed me to live in a time and place where that exists. Graham will step in to help me meet my obligations. I will eventually heal, and get the boot off, and move on with my life."

"That story has a happy ending. You're worried about … other things I'm not sure you should focus on."

"You're right. I'm worried about tragedies. Graham already helped me with one of those. He reminded me that when he dies, he'll be in heaven, and things like estate planning could help any loved ones he left behind. I'd not only have God but also His people for support. I've been so focused on the pain, I never put much thought into the tangible ways God might provide. The reminder was life-giving."

"So you want to work through all your worries that way."

"Sounds like an awful time, doesn't it?" Piper parked in her driveway. Because of her dinner plans, Bryce was at a friend's house this evening. Except for Teddy, she'd have the place to herself to get started. "I'm hopeful, but I'm also worried I'll get bogged down. I could use some supervision."

Lucy chuckled. "I'll be there in twenty."

Chapter Thirty-One

The clock may as well have gone into hibernation for the winter with how slowly it moved. Because another officer was sick with the flu, Graham had gone into work. If the last five minutes of the shift ever ticked away, he'd change and catch the last hour of the auction. Since most of the town would be there, the crowd ought to allow him to avoid Piper, giving her the space they'd agreed to.

Perhaps it'd been a rookie move, asking for a commitment early on instead of seeing where their second chance took them naturally. And maybe telling her to spend a bunch of time thinking about her fears had been a mistake.

For one or both reasons, she might never cash in that raincheck, and the only evidence of him left in her life would be the fingerprint he'd pressed into the coffee table. If she even kept it. When he'd collected the auction pieces that morning and delivered them to the high school, the paint on his special project still hadn't cured. He'd left it in the stockroom.

The last minute of his shift finally ticked away. He headed to the locker room where he'd hung the blue button-down and nice jeans he'd planned to wear to the auction. But maybe he ought to stay in uniform. If stereotypes held true, maybe then Piper wouldn't be able to resist him.

"If you're thinking of skipping, think again."

Graham tilted his head to see around the locker door.

Cody crossed his arms and leaned a shoulder into a pillar in the center of the aisle. He was dressed in jeans, a polo, and a winter jacket, probably fresh from the auction. Graham had texted him earlier that he'd be working until seven, and Cody must've pegged him as a flight risk.

"I'm going. Wanting to support the Rasinskis is how I got into this. I'm not going to give up on them now."

"But you will give up on Piper?"

"If she says we're done, I have nothing left to convince her to stay. I don't get why ..." Emotion sprung up, barricading his throat. Why were the women in his life always abandoning him?

He shook his head. He didn't know what Piper would decide yet. She might not walk away.

Then again, she might.

"God's got you. You have to trust Him with Piper too."

Trust God. He'd urged Piper to do just that. But could he trust God to work things out with Piper? Not necessarily. The Lord might not want them together. If so, God would see him through, but he'd much rather find a way to tip the scales in his favor.

But he'd already tried this his way, and look where it'd gotten him. He'd change out of the uniform. She wouldn't change her mind over something so superficial anyway. Although, she had given that customer advice on what to wear after a breakup. He gulped, wondering what outfit she'd chosen for herself and whether he'd be able to keep a level head around her.

Cody pushed away from the pillar. "I'll see you there?"

"Yeah. Right behind you."

Graham changed and trudged out to his truck. Possibility with Piper had added a certain spark to his days over the last few weeks. The dimming of that light meant even the auction didn't interest him the way it had.

Vehicles packed the high school's lot. Instead of trolling the aisles for a closer spot, Graham pulled up along the curb at the back of the parking area. As he took the keys from the ignition, a group of three boys and a gangly dog stepped from the parking lot into the ballfield. The child with the dog was Bryce, if he wasn't mistaken.

He climbed from the truck and waved hello, but the boys weren't looking. Bryce fell back from the others and turned toward the dog, probably trying to make sure the puppy did what he needed to do before they went back inside.

Though tempted to avoid the event by lingering outside, Graham sighed and turned for the school.

He held the door for a family who was exiting, probably already late for bedtime. The father carried the youngest girl, a three- or four-year-old with tights and black patent leather shoes sticking out from beneath her purple winter coat. The mom rested her hand inside the dad's elbow, steadying herself on some ice, as she held the hand of their son, a kindergartener or first grader.

"How will we know if we won?"

At the excitement in the boy's voice, the little girl lifted her head from her dad's shoulder.

The family continued toward their car, and Graham didn't hear the father's answer. He didn't need to. He'd seen enough to know the family *had* won. They had each other. Meanwhile, thanks to Piper, Graham was left without the woman he loved once again.

But maybe only for now. Maybe the Lord would bring her around.

Maybe.

He pulled open the gym door. Auction items, food and beverage stations, and various activity booths had been set up around the perimeter of the room. The center consisted of round banquet tables covered in shiny silver and gold tablecloths. His eyes tracked to the area where he and Cody had set up the furniture this morning, but Piper didn't stand among the pieces.

But then his vision caught on a woman seated at a table near the display.

Piper wore black heels and a knee-length dress in a similar shade of blue as his own shirt. An image came to mind of her grandparents, Ralph and Gertrude, in their cranberry shirts at Thanksgiving. If people knew they'd been close lately—and of course they knew—they'd think they'd planned to match. They'd be wrong.

He veered right, into a small Christmas tree forest volunteers must've put up. Kids kicked and twirled through the fake snow. Ahead, a little village of booths sold baked treats, crafts, and hot cocoa. Everyone was smiling and laughing.

Everyone but Graham.

Maybe he should find the donation bin, leave his contribution, wish the family well, and head out. He could feel good about having ensured the furniture was ready to go. Even if he didn't get his ideal happy ending, at least he could help the Rasinskis toward theirs.

Chapter Thirty-Two

Piper chewed her lip and rolled her ankle in an ineffective attempt to ease the ache in her foot. She'd been on it way too much today—and in heels, no less. The doctor would not be happy with her. In minutes, she'd know how the bidding had turned out. Then, she could go to bed a happy woman.

In theory.

In reality, she ached as she watched Graham.

She and Lucy had talked for a couple of hours last night, starting and ending with prayer. Working through one what-if after another had been like watching a balloon drain of air until her fears were nothing but a shriveled, easily discarded blob. Afterward, she'd slept more soundly than she had in ages. She wanted to tell Graham about it, but he'd said they could reconnect after Christmas. Would he believe how far she'd come since last night?

For that matter, should *she* trust how far she'd come? The whole reason she'd turned his dinner invitation into a date had been because she'd been as interested in a future together as he was. Then she'd waffled. Turned out, her bad balance extended beyond the physical. She owed it to him to keep her distance until she was sure she had both feet firmly on the ground.

Graham and Cody got into some kind of mild skirmish. Cody seemed to be keeping something away from Graham. Keys? He stuffed the object in his pants pocket and displayed his empty hands. Graham seemed to draw the line at going in his friend's pocket. With a sour look, he followed a triumphant Cody to the arcade games.

"If we're not going to talk about the elephant in the room, what do you want to talk about?" Lucy swirled her punch glass.

Piper forced her focus off Graham to take in her surroundings again. Strings of lights, lavish Christmas trees, fake snow the janitors would probably hate, and festive booths had transformed the gymnasium. Even the punch in Lucy's glass was special. Though Connie Reynolds still wouldn't share her Cowboy Christmas Cider recipe, she had mixed up a big batch for the benefit auction. "The committee really outdid themselves."

"You've already told me that three times."

Riley Rasinski wore a sequined party dress and sat on the floor in front of the throne the volunteers had made for her. A group of giggling girls, also in pretty dresses, surrounded her. Together, the children focused on a game involving cups and little plastic elves.

"She looks so happy."

"You've also commented on that multiple times, but ..." Lucy grinned. "I'll give you that. It doesn't get old, does it? And look at her parents."

The young couple talked with others from the community, all smiles and laughter.

"I'm glad we could be involved." The furniture was one section of a much larger selection. Even pop star Alicia Carver,

171

who was indeed in town, had gotten involved by donating backstage passes to her New Year's Eve show. The concert was yet another charity event, that one benefitting Harvest House, a shelter for abused women and children. The various benefits piggybacking off each other without diminishing any individual cause showcased Redemption Ridge's generosity.

Volunteers collected the bidding clipboards, ending the auction.

Soon, the furniture Graham had worked so hard on would go to new homes. So many memories were tied to them. The time she'd walked back to find him sanding and hope had practically floated off him. The stockroom picnic. Their kiss.

Longing settled in her lungs like dust, and she coughed.

She turned away, and her line of sight landed on Teddy's makeshift pen. Another reminder of Graham. The pen was how she got permission to bring the puppy along—he would be contained, and they'd covered the floor underneath with old blankets to protect the hardwood.

The pen sat empty at the moment. Bryce must have the puppy out somewhere.

"Have you seen Teddy and Bryce recently?"

Lucy frowned, idly scanning the crowd. "Not since he and his friends went outside."

Piper checked the time on her phone. "Wasn't that a while ago? He'd better not be walking him around the gym." She leaned one way and then the other, looking for the pair.

They ought to be easy to spot, but all she found was the two boys Bryce had gone outside with.

"I'll go find him." Lucy stood. "You need to rest your foot."

With a sigh, Piper slouched into her chair. Her gaze wandered to Graham's broad shoulders as he rolled a ball toward the rings and holes at the end of the sloped lane. He must've gotten the score he wanted because he punched both arms up and turned with a smile that melted the moment his gaze hit on her across the room.

He nodded hello, and she waved back.

Maybe it wasn't too soon. She could go over there, start the conversation they needed to have. It was getting late, and he had a long drive first thing in the morning, but surely, for love, he could miss some sleep.

Or perhaps that was selfishness on her part.

Wilhelmina Dobbs stepped up to the microphone to announce the auction winners. The crowd gathered around her, clapping as she revealed the final bids. One piece of furniture after another was awarded to new owners, each paying well over what the pieces were worth.

Lucy cut across the gymnasium toward her. Beyond her, Cody finally gave back whatever he'd taken from Graham. Yep. The item had to be keys. Graham slung on his coat and started for the exit.

"He's not here?" Lucy asked.

"No. He's leaving." Piper tried to dismiss her disappointment. They'd have to talk after Christmas.

"I mean Bryce. The boys said they turned around while they were outside, and he wasn't with them anymore. I asked them to check the boy's bathroom, and I walked around the outside of the school, but he's not here."

Feeling like she was sliding out of control on a patch of ice, Piper braced her hand on the table as she rose. People crowded the room, limiting her view. Or was it panic making it hard to see?

"We should have her ask if anyone's seen him." Lucy stepped toward Wilhelmina as she finished reading off the last winners.

Piper did one more visual pass over the room. Graham was gone, and the longing she'd felt for his company multiplied. She pressed a hand to her stomach. Bryce going missing hadn't been one of the scenarios she and Lucy had run through last night, but given the way he'd skipped school that once, it should've been. Was all her planning for naught?

Lord, it's always come down to You, not my plans. Please show us where Bryce is and guide us, no matter what happens.

Cody and a couple of other officers sat around a table, drinking punch and hot cocoa. Other adults mingled around the auction. Children crisscrossed the room, but no puppies trailed them. Bryce didn't seem to be here. She limped after Lucy, her heart picking up speed and her stomach turning to stone.

Lucy reached Wilhelmina, and her hands moved as she related the story.

"Oh, you poor thing," Wilhelmina said as Piper neared. With a sympathetic smile, she took to the mic again. "Is Bryce Wells in the room? Anyone seen him and the puppy?"

Louder conversations quieted to a murmur out of respect for the announcement, but no one spoke over the noise to point out her nephew.

Piper rubbed her hand over her stomach. He had to be here. She couldn't have lost him.

God, please, have mercy.

Emanuel. God with us, through it all.

Wilhelmina lifted her hand high above her head and snapped. "Excuse me, everyone. We need to find Bryce Wells. Has anyone seen him?"

The increased urgency in Wilhelmina's voice finally hushed the conversations. Faces turned first toward the mic, and then this way and that.

"Anyone? Bryce, are you here?"

Everyone in attendance began to look around. Cody and the other officers rose. After a brief discussion, Cody jogged from the room while a man who looked to be in his fifties or sixties approached Piper.

If only he were Graham.

Lucy wrapped an arm around her, as if sensing she was about to crumple.

Piper hadn't imagined this scenario or how it would play out, but apparently, she was about to find out, one step at a time. Though she longed for Graham, she thanked God for Lucy and the man who came to a stop before her.

"I'm Officer Hughes. Off duty, but ..." Hughes shrugged, took his phone from his pocket, and tapped on the screen a couple of times before focusing a concerned but steady gaze on Piper. "When did you see him last?"

Piper drew a ragged breath. "When he took Teddy outside. It was an hour ago. With the event, I ... I ..." Distracted by the auction and Graham, she'd let Bryce either wander off or ... worse.

Lucy seemed to sense Piper dropping toward an emotional black hole. She squeezed Piper's shoulders. "We thought he was in the room, playing with the other kids and the puppy. He left school once a couple of months ago and went and got himself a cupcake." She dipped her face to speak directly to Piper. "It's probably something equally harmless this time."

Piper kept her head tilted down, and her tears fell to the gym floor. She should've been more vigilant. Should've known better.

Hughes' voice rumbled, overpowering her thoughts. "Did anything happen that might have prompted him to wander off?"

She'd taken Bryce to see his father. He'd been excited on the way there. Ryan had talked with him about how he hadn't played in the state game. Piper had listened and thought he'd done a wonderful job encouraging Bryce to follow through on his place on the team, his obvious skill.

"He found out his dad lied to him." It sounded terrible when she said it. He'd been quiet on the way home, hadn't he?

She'd been distracted by thoughts of Graham most of the day. "I thought he was okay, but maybe ..." Maybe he'd run away over it. He was the boy who'd skipped school for a cupcake on a whim. What would he do over a disappointment like the one he'd gotten today?

"Does he have a cell phone on him?"

"No. He's only ten."

"What was he wearing the last time you saw him?"

Piper described Bryce's coat and Teddy. "You don't think he could've gone far ...?"

"Your number?"

Piper recited it, and Hughes typed on his phone.

After a couple more questions, he stepped back. "I'll call it in. I'll ask an officer to meet you at your house to check if he's there. Call his friends' parents too."

Piper nodded, numb. Most of Bryce's friends and their families milled about in the gymnasium, and her house was too far from the high school for Bryce to have walked there. Still, the tasks would help her feel less useless.

Hughes gave a tight smile. "We'll find him. If he turns up or you think of anything else, call the precinct."

As he strode away, Lucy rubbed her back. "I'll drive you."

"Okay." What else could she say?

As Graham had promised, God was providing in tangible ways. It didn't feel like enough, but she had the support she needed to take the next step. She'd take it in faith that the Lord would also provide for the step after that.

If only she could lean on Graham's arm as she took them.

Chapter Thirty-Three

Adrenaline pulsed through Graham, but he kept his breathing even, his focus on the road. Piper had to be beside herself, but if he was going to help locate Bryce, he needed to keep his head.

Because he'd seen the boy outside with Teddy, Graham was one of the last to know his location. If he'd stopped to talk to Bryce, they might not be in this mess. But then again, Bryce could've simply said he was taking care of Teddy, and he would've had no reason to doubt him.

He scanned the street as he drove back to the school but saw no signs of the boy or the puppy. He pulled into the same spot he'd vacated a few minutes ago and hopped down. Cody, who'd called to tell him what had happened, rounded a vehicle to appear at his side.

"I saw him over here." Graham grabbed the flashlight from the toolbox behind his seat and flipped it on.

"Got another one?" Cody lifted his cell phone. The flashlight app would only cover a couple of steps ahead once they got away from the glow of the parking area.

"Sorry."

"Okay. Where was he?"

Graham jogged to the spot, Cody following. Together, they peered at the ground.

Today's sun had evaporated the last traces of snow. The schoolyard's grass had been worn thin, the dirt beneath pounded flat by the many who walked around out here every day.

"Not the easiest place to track a person," Cody muttered.

"They were headed this way, last I saw." Graham continued in the direction he'd seen the pair walking until he reached the edge of the school property. From there, scraggly grass poked as high as his knees, dotted with sagebrush and juniper. Ahead, a stretch of aspens and pines marked an undeveloped area around a creek that wound through part of town. This stretch of woods extended about half a city block wide and two long. Plenty of room for a ten-year-old to get turned around.

Graham turned a slow circle, looking for any signs Bryce had come this way. Wandering into the natural area wasn't the path of least resistance, but if the kid wanted to hide, he might've continued. But had he?

An odor cut through the crisp scents of juniper and sage. After some trial and error, he discovered a little pile of dog droppings on a deer trail a couple of feet into the natural area.

He motioned Cody over. "They came this way."

Cody shined his phone light ahead, but the device did little to reveal the subtle path as it extended farther from the lights by the school.

"If they came this far, they might've kept following the trail." Graham's flashlight provided more illumination but didn't reveal the boy or give much information about the direction the footpath took. That, he'd have to discover a couple of steps at a time, even in broad daylight.

"I'll head back, let the others know, and upgrade this."

Cody lifted the ineffective light once more and turned toward the school.

Swinging his light side to side to scan for spur trails or the boy himself, Graham followed the narrow path into the woods. Brush raked against his clothing as branches overhead blocked the moonlight, turning the passage into a tunnel.

This would be a scary place for a child in the dark. Scary enough that he might want a rescuer. "Bryce?"

At a rustle, Graham froze. Skittering that started at ground level and rose overhead suggested the source was an animal, not a child.

A few feet later, the ground softened, and the path opened into the creek bed. Graham scanned the muddy earth at the edge, non-stop prayers running through his mind. The stream was only four or five inches deep, but several feet across. Thanks to its constant movement and daytime temperatures above freezing, the water hadn't turned to ice. But after dark like this, the air had dipped into the twenties, and wandering around wet could lead to hypothermia. Hopefully, they hadn't waded through.

The scents of dirt and pine floated lightly on the frozen air. The calls of others echoed from behind him, and he tried shouting the boy's name again, but to no avail. The puppy was more loyal to Graham, however, and might give their location away.

"Teddy! Here, boy! Come here!"

No response.

He combed the edge of the creek. A variety of footprints meant kids from the school hung out back here, obscuring any hope of finding Bryce's prints. Then, right at the edge of the water, the mud outlined a fresh paw print. Dark splotches on the far bank suggested someone had tracked moisture up from the stream.

Bryce and Teddy had crossed here.

With no bridge in sight, Graham splashed into the stream. Icy water flooded his shoes in the two seconds it took him to cross. Hopefully, Bryce had carried Teddy when they'd faced the obstacle, because having cold feet was bad enough. On the puppy, the water would've come up higher.

They needed to find them.

God, help us.

He texted Cody an update and scanned for his next clue, praying there would be one. The damp trail ended where the brush began, but the overgrown grass had been pressed down. Not an often-used deer trail this time, but something more temporary and fragile—like what a kid might leave when he trampled through.

He hesitated, completing another scan for other possibilities. Seeing none that looked as likely, he followed the thin evidence in a path parallel to the creek but about ten feet into the brush. Was this really the way? Staying at the edge of the creek would've offered a clearer path.

He stopped, called out, and turned again. Neither Bryce nor Teddy responded. Presumably following the information Graham provided through Cody, other searchers weren't far behind him, combing the area. If Graham was on the wrong track, hopefully someone else was on the right one.

But, wow, he wanted to be the one to reunite Bryce with Piper.

He continued until a light appeared through the branches. A street. The boy would be harder to track on a sidewalk—if Graham was even on the trail anymore—but at least he'd be more likely to be seen by the public.

A low bridge—flat at street level—allowed the street to pass over the stream. The grass running along the structure to the street had been matted down, but by what? Rain and melting snow or Bryce and Teddy?

If he'd really been determined to hide, Bryce might've

crawled under the low bridge. Graham flashed his light beneath. Cobwebs and decaying leaves caught the light, but the glow revealed no signs of the boy or dog. The pillar-like abutments might offer space for a child to squeeze out of view, but in such a creepy setting?

Bryce would've chosen the sidewalk.

Graham climbed the incline and scanned the street. A dentist's office, a small bank, and houses lined the areas beyond the sidewalks. No one moved in the glow of the street-lights or the illuminated parking areas. Then again, even if Bryce had come this way, he could be long gone by now. Hopefully to someplace he and the dog could get warm and dry. A breeze sighed through the trees, and water gurgled beneath the bridge.

A more distinct splash rose. And then rustling indicated an animal. A squirrel?

Graham half-walked, half-slid back down to the bank of the stream and waited.

More rustling.

He turned toward the noise. Someone or something was under the bridge.

Another scuffle.

And then a small, rumbly bark. The kind Teddy used to voice frustration when his toy had rolled out of reach.

Graham crouched and shined his flashlight beneath the bridge. This time, something moved about halfway back, a foot or a tail sticking out and rustling the leaves. "Hey, Bryce. How are you guys doing under there?"

No answer.

Graham dropped to his knees, preparing to crawl under, and moisture soaked through his jeans. A sniffle reached him as he ducked his head under the structure. Another rustle, and a shape bounded toward him.

Teddy. Dry and exuberant. Graham grabbed the leash.

Either Bryce had been considerate, or the dog had been wisely uncooperative about splashing into the stream. Whatever the case, the puppy hadn't waded through.

As soon as the puppy finished licking his face in greeting, he continued toward the sneaker poking out from behind an abutment. "You all right, Bryce?"

"Leave me alone." The boy's foot pulled back, but the response sent a wave of relief over Graham. If nothing else, Bryce was responsive. The boy had hunkered down between two pillars, his knees to his chest.

Graham felt like a contortionist as he positioned himself next to him. "Everyone's worried and looking. Are you okay?"

"I'm fine." His teeth clicked. Chattering? "Leave me alone."

"I can't. You must be wet from crossing the stream. It's dangerous to stay out in the cold like that." To keep Teddy from wandering into the water, he pulled the dog onto his lap, then unzipped his coat and shrugged it off. He slipped his phone from the jacket pocket, then fit the garment around Bryce's shivering shoulders.

That done, he needed to inform everyone of their location. Though he was tempted to take the extra time to message Piper, he instead used his most recent message thread. As soon as Cody got the message, he'd direct the searchers and be on the phone with her.

Graham sent the text then refocused. "Why are we under here?"

"Nobody cares about me."

"That's not true. Half the town is out looking for you." Concern and the hike through the woods had warmed Graham, but without his coat, the heat evaporated. Already, he could feel the chill raising goosebumps on his neck. And his feet felt like ice cubes.

"My dad lied to me. Nobody loves me."

Ah. Piper had said Ryan was going to talk to him today about his basketball track record. The conversation must've happened—and hit Bryce square in the heart. "He did lie to you, and I'm sure he feels terrible. But that doesn't mean he doesn't love you. Sometimes, people who love us make mistakes." Even as he spoke, he thought of Piper.

But did she love him? That was one of the questions he'd asked her to consider.

"He wouldn't be in jail if he loved me."

"Why do you think so?"

"Because if he loved me more than he loved drugs, he wouldn't have broken the law and got put in prison where I can't be with him. He would've chosen me."

"He didn't love drugs. He was addicted." Graham could still picture the man's gaunt body and hollowed-out face when he'd surrendered from behind the wheel of the stolen car. "Do you know what that means?"

Bryce shrugged.

"Once some people start with drugs, it's like being sick. They'll do anything to feel better and don't realize their actions hurt people they love. That's why we try so hard to stop people from trying drugs in the first place. It can be really hard to make good choices."

"Dad didn't make good choices. He didn't choose me. Why didn't he like me enough? What did I do wrong?"

As if he could sense Bryce's heartbreak, Teddy squirmed toward him, and Graham gave him slack on the leash. The dog wedged his nose under Bryce's hand, and the boy clutched the puppy into a hug.

Time for a different tack. A more personal one. "My parents got a divorce when I was nine. Dad was still around, but I wasn't much older than you are the last time I talked to my mom. She didn't choose me either." His throat surprised him by turning scratchy and thick.

Bryce peered at him, eyes wide and glossy in the glow of the flashlight.

No going back. The kid was counting on him.

Maybe there was still something here he needed to face for himself too. "There's nothing we can do to make people choose us."

Graham would know. After his mom told him staying in touch was too hard for her, he'd called again and again until someone else had answered her number—she'd changed hers without offering him the new one. Through the years, part of him had hoped that if he performed well enough in sports or school or at the academy or on the job, she might hear about him, might be proud enough to reconnect. After he'd joined the police force, he'd dug up her information, but when he'd called, she'd told him to leave her alone. None of those efforts had worked because her decision had never been within his ability to control.

"People might not choose us, but that doesn't mean we did something wrong." As he spoke, an idea occurred to him, one he hadn't tied into the rejections in his own life before. "The only perfect person to ever live was rejected by a lot of people."

"Jesus?"

Graham nodded. Piper had once said he needed to forgive his mom, and only now did he realize why he'd had such a hard time with that—he'd also needed to forgive himself for not being someone she'd chosen. As he took that first step, the second—dropping the bitterness toward his mother—finally became possible.

Perhaps he'd expected to impress Piper into choosing him too. He'd been blindsided when she'd refused his proposal, angry at himself and her. But her decision had been about her fears—fears that still might steal her away. If so, he'd have to forgive both himself and her. But her request for a raincheck wasn't a rejection. Not yet anyway.

Just like Ryan's lie wasn't meant to leave Bryce feeling unloved.

He glanced over at Bryce. "Sometimes, even people who love us choose wrong. Your father, for example, loves you very much. I think if you tell him how hurt you are by his choices, he'll tell you how sorry he is."

"Sorry isn't good enough."

"Still hurts, huh?"

Bryce's pout deepened toward a scowl.

"I hear you. Everyone but God is going to let us down sometimes, and it's going to hurt. But we can still get glimpses of real love through other relationships. I think that's one reason God gave you such a great aunt. She isn't perfect, but she loves you."

"She loves *you*."

A wordless prayer, more of a hope pointed heavenward that that might be true, swelled in his chest. "I don't know if she does, but I *do* know she asked everyone she could to help find you." Graham pointed Bryce's attention toward the flashlights, blinking through the trees as the search party caught up to them.

Bryce's mouth opened in a silent "Oh."

"She was on her way to check your house for you, but I bet she's speeding over here as we speak."

Bryce shrank back into the shadows. "Are you going to arrest her?"

"No." Graham laughed, loud and light. He'd needed this talk at least as much as Bryce had. "If I were with her, I'd help her get here as fast as possible."

"You'd use your lights and sirens?"

"The whole nine yards. Let's go out there and meet her. Follow me, okay?"

Chapter Thirty-Four

"There." Piper thumped the window of Lucy's car, and her friend braked. Cody's call had said Bryce had been hiding under the Eighth Street bridge. Piper had never even realized there was a bridge on Eighth, but flashlights shone from among the trees at the side of the road.

As soon as the car stopped, Piper jumped out and hurried toward the lights. Sure enough, a low bridge supported the road over a small creek. She steadied herself with a hand on the concrete structure as she stepped down the decline. Thankfully, when they'd stopped home, she'd thought to change out of the heels and into her thick-soled shoes so she could search.

She paused partway down to look ahead. In the focus of the lights stood a man with a boy at his side. Bryce, looking as bulky as a snowman under an extra winter coat, held Graham's hand.

Tears pressed hard as she returned her focus to her balance. By the time she'd descended the slope, she was sniffling. Despite the throb in her foot, she ran and wrapped her arms around Bryce.

She gripped him tight. "Never, never, never, never do that again."

"I'm sorry." Her coat muffled his words.

She held him at arm's distance, and the extra coat that had been around his shoulders dropped to the ground. As Graham replaced it over Bryce, she realized it was his. She offered him a smile that came nowhere close to expressing her gratitude before refocusing on Bryce. "Are you okay?"

Dirt smeared his cheek and neck, but he nodded and passed his hand under his nose. Apparently, she wasn't the only one overcome by emotion. "Coach Graham found me."

She pulled Bryce into a second hug but lifted her gaze to Graham. In the glow from the others' lights, she could see his mussed-up hair, the leaf stuck to his shoulder, the dirt and moisture on the legs of his jeans. As the others passed by to use the sidewalk to return to the school, he stayed motionless, watching the reunion while Teddy wriggled in his arms. What a picture he made, a true hero.

Her hero.

Bryce's sniffles redirected her.

"Let's get you warmed up. Come on. Lucy's here." She gently nudged Bryce toward the road, then looked back to Graham. Should she take Teddy? Could they possibly have their talk tonight instead of after Christmas? Because going their separate ways sounded like misery. "Thank you."

The words seemed inadequate.

"You're welcome." He motioned her to follow Bryce toward the street, but she couldn't.

"I thought you'd gone home for the night."

"I was on my way there when I got the call."

"You didn't have to come back."

"Of course I did."

"But, after everything ..." She bit her lip. She'd pushed Graham away. Repeatedly.

"After everything, you should know I'm not going to stand by when I could be helping." He stepped closer and motioned again for her to precede him up the incline. "You need to get these two home and warmed up."

She made her way back to the street, taking care not to trip. Bryce climbed ahead into the warm car. Graham passed him the puppy, and Piper shut them in. They couldn't leave until she retook her seat, but she couldn't stand to abandon Graham without saying something about how she was glad he'd been there. Something about how she'd seen God's faithfulness tonight. How even as one of her worst nightmares seemed to be coming true, He'd provided all the support she could've asked for—in part, through Graham. And whatever life had in store, she'd rather face it with Graham than without for as long as God would give them together.

Why did her tongue seem frozen?

Graham looked down the sidewalk, after the others on their way back to the school and their vehicles.

"The auction went well," she said. "We raised a lot of money for the Rasinskis."

"I'm sure we did." Graham lifted a hand; a goodbye wave, she realized. He planned to walk with everyone else.

"You're the hero. The least we can do is give you a lift back."

"No, thanks. It's not far." He turned and started down the sidewalk.

* * *

Not getting in the car, not spending one evening acting like everything between them was better, was the hardest thing he'd done in years. He cared about Piper and Bryce. He'd do anything to ensure their safety and happiness—including walk away when he knew Piper would be glad he had. If she'd needed time after the robbery, she'd require even more now. After all, scary events had never led the Piper he knew to feel more at peace. Quite the opposite.

"Graham, wait."

His feet drew to a stop.

She caught up and touched his arm as she circled to stand in front of him. "If you'd been injured in the robbery, the whole police force wouldn't have been able to keep me from your hospital room. I would've kept you company until you healed. I imagine there's lots of paperwork associated with doctors and work leaves, and we both know I have more patience for that kind of thing, so I would've helped. I would've nagged you about rehab if you'd been assigned exercises. I would've taken you to dinner to celebrate when you were able to return to full duty—because we both know cooking is more your thing." She bit her lip, her eyes glimmering with hope.

She'd done what he'd asked. She'd thought through the steps of what would happen if one of her fears had come true. And instead of focusing on losses and what couldn't be, she'd stuck to the practicalities.

She'd chosen him.

She'd chosen him, right? Before he could find the words to ask, she grabbed his hand. "Could you stop over? I do need to get Bryce to bed, but then, I'd really like to talk with you. I know you said after Christmas, but ..."

How was he supposed to say no? "I'll see you soon."

Her shoulders lifted with giddy joy, and a noise somewhere between a laugh and a squeak of delight slipped from her throat. She clamped a hand over her mouth.

He chuckled. "I'll give you a little while to talk to him."

"Okay." She hurried off, and Graham continued to the school.

Inside, he changed into his dry work pants, socks, and

boots. When he came back out, Cody walked up. Though Graham was anxious to finish his conversation with Piper, he spent the next half an hour chatting with Cody to allow her time to get Bryce to bed.

When he finally pulled up to her house, lights shined warmly through the windows, but that was nothing compared to the warmth of the smile she offered as she let him in.

"How is Bryce?" he asked.

"Tucked in, snug and warm. I'll have a longer talk with him tomorrow, but for now, I tried to make sure he knows how loved he is." Energy radiating off her, she probably didn't even notice the limp that suggested she'd overdone it tonight as she stepped back into her living room. But instead of inviting him to sit, she turned back toward him. "About what I said about taking on the police force to see you ..."

Was he allowed to laugh? Because that did form quite the image.

She chuckled. "For the record, I don't think the police would've tried to stop me from being by your side. Because one of the gifts God's given me is this wonderful community. The people of Redemption Ridge saw me through the loss of my parents. Sometimes, it felt like there was never the same amount of love and joy after they died, but part of the reason for that was the way I walled people off. I didn't let many people close. So, family and friends and the community get a role in the answers to all my what-ifs.

"I hope you'll let me have a role in the answers to all the what-ifs I've asked about you. Like, 'What if you get sick?' I hope the answer is I get to be your nurse. And if you get hurt, I hope I get to be your support. And if you are still open to a future together, I hope to discover it with you."

His hands found their way to her arms, resting gently on her shoulders. "You're really ... Are you sure?"

She nodded, bit her lips together, and nodded again.

"Tonight, having you and so many other officers to turn to when I needed help ... I saw how important your job is. I'm beyond grateful for what you do and proud to know a man who helps people on their worst days. So, if you need me, Graham, I'm going to be right here. By your side. The way you've been here for me."

He touched her jaw. The warmth of her skin signaled that his fingers were too cold to touch her. He was about to pull back when Piper covered his hands with hers, allowing him to touch her neck and cheeks without flinching at the cold.

He studied her lips. Those were probably warm and soft too. "This isn't just the emotions of getting Bryce back?"

"I thought it through. The truth became clear when I faced my fears instead of trying to push them away. I'm sure I'll have moments in the future, but I'm done being crippled by worry." Without disturbing his touch on her neck, she lowered her hands to his sides, moving close enough that her dress whispered against his button-down. "There's only one what-if I can't answer on my own."

He brushed his thumb over the edge of her mouth. "Which is?"

The corners of her lips quirked. "What if I told you I love you?"

He hooked his finger under her chin and lowered his lips to hers. She was warm, her mouth soft against his as her arms tightened around his waist. He threaded his fingers into her hair, keeping her close, making up for lost time.

Allowing a sliver of space, he brushed her cheek again. "I love you too."

"Aside from Jesus, you're the best thing to ever happen to me, Graham Lockhart."

He managed to squelch his grin long enough to brush another kiss across those lips. As they parted again, he took her hand. "What if you and Bryce came with me over Christmas?"

"Let's see …" She pressed her lips together in thought, her expression so cute, he almost interrupted with another kiss. "We'd have to scramble to get ready, but I bet Lucy would watch Teddy. We'd have to postpone our plans with my grandparents, but I think they'd understand. Although they and your family would probably assume we were very serious about each other."

"And what if we are?"

This time, she tightened her arms around his neck, pulling him down as she went up on tiptoes to press a quick peck to his lips. "Sounds like the best-case scenario."

Epilogue

What if it was too soon?

Piper's what-if questions had lost most of their bluster, but this one got her heart going.

Graham laid his hand over hers where it rested in the crook of his elbow. Though he didn't voice a question, his glance conveyed concern.

The hostess had moved ahead of them into the dining room of Ridgeline Grill, but worried mess she was, Piper had failed to follow. With a sheepish smile, she quick-stepped to catch back up. Graham squeezed her hand in reassurance as they threaded into the maze of tables.

Off to the right, near the door to the kitchen, sat Jason Keen. A few months ago, when she'd had her untimely run-in with a pickup truck, Jason had been the one to drive her to the doctor. Tonight, he sat with his arm around his wife, Cassie, discussing what looked to be serious matters with Cassie's brothers. Made sense, what with them all in business together as the owners of this restaurant and the ranch it sat on. But the part that stood out to her and spoke to her what-if question was the sweet way Jason paid attention when his wife spoke.

By all accounts, Jason and Cassie had gotten married quickly. Maybe even—according to some people—too quickly.

And closer to her own table, Mav and Bella Knight dined. Again, not people Piper knew well personally, but their marriage had been through the wringer too, and look at both couples now. Happy. Committed.

So, what if it was too soon to propose to Graham? If he did say yes, even prematurely, the Lord could still work things out.

Besides, maybe she and Graham had only reconnected a couple of months ago, but they'd dated a year in the past. She knew him, and he knew her. And he'd already said he was all in.

The hostess started to pull out her chair for her, but Graham took over. He squeezed her shoulder before taking the seat across the small table from her. As he got situated, his gaze roamed their surroundings. Not unusual for him. First, this place was packed with memories, not all of them good. Second, as a police officer, he cataloged more details than she'd ever notice.

Ridgeline Grill wasn't formal, but it was one of the nicer restaurants in Redemption Ridge. Exposed beams and antler chandeliers dressed down the creamy linen tablecloths. The dress code, if you could call it that, varied from casual to semi-dressy, sometimes even among those sharing a table.

For example, Bethany Shepherd, who owned the local bookstore, wore jeans and a slouchy cardigan. With her sat Margie Buchannan. The real estate agent wore sharp black pants and a jewel-tone blazer. Nearby, lawyer Ruby Thompson had dressed to kill, trading her usual professional attire for an elegant red dress. Her husband, Levi, had made an effort by choosing a black button-down, but he hadn't upgraded his jeans and cowboy boots. Not that Ruby seemed to mind—she only had eyes for her man.

Speaking of ... Piper refocused.

The blue-gray of Graham's sweater brought out his eyes. He pushed up his sleeves as he finished his scan of the room and lifted his menu. He must've thought he'd cleared the dining room of threats, but he apparently hadn't thought to read much into his date.

Her face burned as she considered the surprise she was planning. She lifted her own menu, but another what-if crashed into her concentration. What if this was the wrong place for a proposal because of the past?

This was their second time back to Ridgeline Grill together since his failed proposal. She eyed the table where it'd happened, currently occupied by famous best friends Clint Taylor and Nora St. James. Instead of sitting across from each other as most of the couples in the room had, the friends sat on adjacent sides of the small, square table, heads tipped together as Clint animatedly recounted some story that had Nora laughing.

Piper and Graham could have a similarly nice time if she dropped this idea of proposing. He'd never know the difference. Eventually, he'd get around to it himself.

Or she could propose somewhere else. But he'd taken her here for their first date. She figured that was why he'd proposed here. The failed proposal had made their first visit back a little awkward at first, but by the end of the meal, they'd been talking and laughing like old times.

"What are you getting?" Graham asked.

She scanned the menu without reading a word. She fell back on what she'd ordered when they'd come here on New Year's Day, three weeks ago. "The petite filet mignon."

"Not going to mess with success, huh?" He tapped his finger against his menu. "I think you should branch out."

She hoisted a coy smile. "Want me to pick something more expensive?"

"I want to make sure you've considered all your options, and I can tell you haven't even read your menu."

How did he read her so well? He hadn't even been looking at her. Or had he? She was so distracted, she couldn't say with any confidence. She blinked hard and forced herself to read the menu.

Appetizers. The meals here were hearty enough that she didn't usually bother with appetizers. She moved on to main courses. There'd either been a shortage tonight or a menu change recently, because a piece of paper had been taped over two of the usual listings. Replacing them was a dish called ... *A Lifetime of Love?*

She read it twice, but the dish name didn't change. Maybe they were testing something out before Valentine's Day? She glanced over at the family in charge of the place. Did a dish name like this really come out of such a serious conversation? She ran her finger beneath the words, a breath away from asking Graham what he thought.

But as she read the description, her lungs stopped working altogether.

Piper and Graham, the ultimate pairing, married with faith in God and accompanied by generous servings of loyalty, appreciation, and commitment, free refills daily.

* * *

Graham watched as Piper's jaw popped open wider and wider, while her lips spread into a grin. He'd seen a no, so he had a pretty good idea how to spot those coming. This was a yes if he'd ever seen one.

Beyond her, Bryce gave him a thumbs up. Gertrude and Ralph beamed. If she hadn't been in such a distracted mood, she might've noticed them enter a minute behind them. She also didn't seem to have noticed Lucy slip into a seat at Mav and Bella Knight's table, where she'd have a clear view to snap pictures of this.

A gutsy choice on his part, maybe, to involve family, to risk rejection in front of a roomful of witnesses once again. But Piper was different than she'd been two years ago.

Without fear holding her back, she'd been connecting on a more meaningful level not only with him, but with a widening circle of friends. They'd been attending a Bible study at church these last few weeks and had enjoyed going deep with the discussions there. Each weekend, she scheduled some event with family or friends—and sometimes both—so elaborate that it took them both to follow through.

One of those nights, when Graham had hosted a shared meal, she'd told him she liked his house. And then, over the next week, she'd redecorated it into the home it'd never been before. Cody's living room looked thrown together in comparison.

As they'd cleaned up after meals and game nights, they'd dreamed about their future. Turned out, without the long shadows cast by what-ifs, she wanted three kids. He'd had two in mind, but that was a compromise he was happy to agree to.

He loved this woman. He wanted to share life with her.

Tears lined her eyes as she looked up from the menu. "Are you asking me to marry you?"

"What if I am?"

She gave a shaky laugh. "Um ..." She swiped under her left eye, even though her tears hadn't spilled over. Then, her hands both disappeared below the table. "You weren't supposed to do this."

He held himself outwardly still as his heart did a swan dive. Not again.

Her eyes went wide. "I mean, that's not a no. It's just ..."

Something thumped onto the floor.

"Oh no." Piper pushed her chair back from the table and leaned sideways but couldn't reach whatever it was.

What in the world was happening? He glanced at Lucy, who had the best chance of offering insight. Mav and Bella both sat, leaned back in their seats with entertained smiles on their faces as they let their food get cold. Seated at their table, Lucy had her phone up and pointed their way, as though instead of taking pictures, she was recording video. She nodded when she noticed Graham looking her way.

She thought this was all right?

He refocused on Piper in time to see her dip below the table—or try to anyway. Another thump, this one the dull thwap of a body part against the wooden furniture, was followed by a muted, "Ow."

Enough already. He was supposed to take a knee, anyway.

He slid from his seat to the floor and lifted the tablecloth to find Piper underneath, one hand pressed to her temple where she must've hit the table, and the other reaching for a metallic mound closer to him than to her.

"I'll get it."

"No. You can't." Piper stopped holding her head to crawl toward him. She claimed the item first, then lifted it to him. "I was going to ask you."

"To tell you the time?"

"No." She giggled. "I'm really flustered. This is ridiculous, right? We should reconvene." She pointed up, still chuckling.

"We probably should, but let's be honest. The traditional proposal went out the window two years ago." He ducked under the tablecloth and joined her under the table. He opened his left hand for the item she held—a man's watch. "What were you going to ask me?"

She chewed her bottom lip, focused on the watch. "You ..." She lifted her line of sight to meet his. "You, Graham Lockhart, are my favorite what-if. What if he loves me? What if we start a family? What if we grow old and gray and happier than we can even imagine together? Thanks to you, I'm not afraid anymore." She scooted closer and gripped his hands around the watch. "When I fall, you catch me. When I crawl under a table during our proposal, you follow me. When I worry, you point me back to God. I'd be most grateful if you'd allow me to spend the rest of my life doing those things in return for you. Will you marry me?"

He turned his right hand, revealing the ring he held between his thumb and pointer finger. "You are my favorite what-if too. Your creativity and your generosity inspire me. Like you've made my house a home, with you, my life is full of warmth and love. Will you marry me?"

She held out her hand so he could slide the ring on. "Yes."

"Then I'll marry you too."

Her shoulders shuddered with a shiver of joy, and she helped secure the watch around his wrist. Hands linked, he leaned in for their first kiss as an engaged couple. The sweet moment lasted until footsteps and a pair of all-black sneakers —probably one of the servers—passed their table.

Piper's breath fluttered against his cheek as she resumed giggling. "You know what the problem with an under-the-table proposal is."

"We have to crawl out of here and face a room full of people."

With a laughing smile, she nodded.

"Together?" he asked.

"Always."

He lifted the tablecloth, and they exited their makeshift privacy. He helped her to her feet as Clint Taylor started a slow clap. All around the restaurant, their family, friends, and acquaintances—the people they didn't know at all, even— grinned at them.

He lifted her hand. "She said yes."

"He said yes," Piper declared at the same time.

The clapping turned into outright applause, but as Graham turned back to Piper and gathered her in his arms for another kiss, his attention did what it'd been doing for months. Years, even. It tunneled down until there was only one person who mattered: Piper Wells.

Ready for more?

Return to Redemption Ridge!

More heartwarming stories are coming in 2024.
In the meantime, join all the fun at our Facebook Reader
Group
www.facebook.com/groups/freedomridgereaders
for sneak peeks, giveaways, and tons of Christmas romance
fun!

Christmas in Redemption Ridge Series

Year 1
Marrying the Rancher's Daughter
(Jason and Cassie)
By Tara Grace Ericson

Remembering the Rancher
(Maverick and Annabella)
By Liwen Ho

Year 2
Amending the Christmas Contract
(Levi and Ruby)
By Hannah Jo Abbott

Wooing the Widower
(Chaz and Margie)
By Elle E Kay

Year 3
Dreaming About Forever
(Jordan and Alicia)
By Mandi Blake

Bidding on a Second Chance
(Graham and Piper)
By Emily Conrad

Heroes of Freedom Ridge Series

Looking for more stories with Christmas, community, and sweet happily ever afters? Visit Freedom Ridge and discover eighteen more faith-filled stories of Christmas in Colorado!

A sweet small-town romance exclusively for Emily's email subscribers.

Food trailer owner Asher has seen too many tears he couldn't dry. Determined to be part of the solution, he avoids romance and all the heartbreaking drama that comes along with it.

At least, that's the plan until his heart decides it has a mind of its own. If he can't rein it in, he's destined to break not one, but two women's hearts.

Sign up for email newsletters at emilyconradauthor.com and receive *Between The Two of Us*, the prequel novella to the Rhythms of Redemption Romances, as a welcome gift.

Also By Emily Conrad

The Rhythms of Redemption Romances

To Bring You Back

An Awestruck Christmas Medley

To Belong Together

To Begin Again

To Believe in You

The Many Oaks Romances

Now or Never

A Surefire Love

Did you enjoy this book?

**Help others discover it by leaving a review on Goodreads
and the site you purchased from!**

Acknowledgments

As always, I have a list of people to thank for their help with this story. Chief among them is my mom.

On October 18th, 2018, I received a text from her that said, "No alarm but I was just hit by a pick up truck in the Aldi parking lot and I'm at the walk in clinic."

It is with her permission that I've used a similar situation (and text) to bring Graham and Piper back together.

The fact that I received that text five years ago and am only just now publishing this story might give you glimpse into how long the process can be to bring a story from idea to published novel.

To my mom and the rest of my family, thank you for sharing this dream with me and cheering me along every step of the way. I couldn't do this without you!

Thank you, Tara Grace Ericson and the rest of the Christmas in Redemption Ridge authors, for inviting me to join you in this series! It's an honor and a joy to participate.

Thank you to my editor, Brandi Aquino, and my professional proofreader, Judi DeVries, for your help polishing Graham and Piper's story.

To my beta readers and volunteer proofreading team, Jessica, Danielle, Jane, Maria, and Teresa, thank you for taking the time to read and share your feedback. Thank you even more for your friendship and support over the years.

Readers, thank you for spending time with Graham and Piper. Some of you have been hanging out in this story universe for years through the Heroes of Freedom Ridge series. Some of you have been following my work through my other stories. Some of you came into this with neither. Whatever the case, you may have risked trying a new-to-you author or series, and I'm so grateful. I hope this story has been a blessing.

And finally, Lord, thank You for being there in every what-if, so that whether I have a plan or not, I can rest assured that I'm safe with You.

About the Author

Emily Conrad writes contemporary Christian romance that explores life's relevant questions. Though she likes to think some of her characters are pretty great, the ultimate hero of her stories (including the one she's living) is Jesus. She lives in Wisconsin with her husband, an energetic coonhound rescue, and two lop-ear bunnies. Learn more about her and her books at emilyconradauthor.com.

 facebook.com/emilyconradauthor

 instagram.com/emilyrconrad